THE LAST HURDLE

GREGORY JOHNSTON

THE LAST HURDLE

A STORY OF ANGUISH
AND HEALING.

ACKNOWLEDGEMENT

| v |

I would like to give a special thanks to my daughter, Reena Johnston, in helping me with this book. She gave me some really good tips and edited my work in the rough draft phases that helped in successfully completing The Last Stand.

Secondly! I would like to thank the people who shared their stories that made this story possible. I can't share their names but they know who they are and I appreciate what they did for me.

Cover photo courtesy of the author, Gregory Johnston.

I

A NOTE FROM THE AUTHOR.

The Last Hurdle is about depression, tragedy, and triumph. Whether you have battled depression from abuse or a tragic loss, or you know someone who has, you can use this book as a stepping stone on the road to recovery.

Depression usually has no signs that are immediately recognizable. For some people, seeing the signs may mean it is too late.

If The Last Hurdle can help even one person overcome their depression and turn themselves around like the characters Shelly and Brooke, then I will consider this book a huge success.

Gregory Johnston

"There is no point treating a depressed person as though she were just feeling sad, saying, 'There now, hang on, you'll get over it.' Sadness is more or less like a head cold- with patience, it passes. Depression is like cancer."

Barbara Kingsolver, The Bean Trees

"Mental pain is less dramatic than physical pain, but it is more common and also more hard to bear. The frequent attempt to conceal mental pain increases the burden: it is easier to say "My tooth is aching" than to say "My heart is broken.""

C.S. Lewis, The Problem of Pain

Once you choose hope, anything's possible
Christopher Reeve

II

THE JOURNEY BEGINS

On the lower level of the Amtrak train, Shelly Murphy stared outside the window from her seat. She paid little attention to the scenery passing by the window. Shelly covered herself in a small lap sized red blanket and propped her head up by a travel pillow. Once she was situated, she raised her legs and rested her feet on the small suitcase she brought to visit her fifty-nine-year-old son, Gary, in Idaho.

In her chair on the Empire Builder Line, as the farm fields and houses whizzed by her window, Shelly wondered why she was making this trip. Shelly has done a lot throughout her life and has been through several hardships.

At one point, it was a lifelong dream—riding the train

across the country for the adventure and nostalgia. This time, Shelly didn't quite feel up to it.

Unfortunately, Shelly had been feeling lonely and unworthy before the journey. Jason Murphy, her second husband of over forty years, passed away from cancer three years prior. A few months after Jason died, Shelly had to move to a different apartment. She could not bear to stay in the one where Jason had passed. Shelly found a small apartment in the town where her youngest daughter, Melanie, lived. She likes her apartment and the people, but she sometimes feels they are too much. They sometimes visit when she does not want company, even at night. The neighbors mean well, but she doesn't want to upset them. Shelly never turns them away.

Shelly thought back to being alone in her apartment, sitting in her recliner, speaking to God. *God, I have nothing more to live for in my old age. I am ready for you to take me when you are ready.* For Shelly, it was all that mattered this time in her life: to have somebody care for her until the end. She was tired of deciding things for herself and others.

She had taken care of kids her entire life. There were her own kids, Jesse, Liz, Gary, and Melanie, and foster kids and kids at her daycare.

Part of the way through her marriage with Jason, they took in foster kids. She had done most of the paperwork and the care-taking for the children. Shelly and Jason watched foster kids for stays up to one year and housed kids for a night or two in emergencies. Thankfully, Shelly kept photos of all the children that stayed with them for a longer period. She sometimes looks at those photos.

Several years later, Shelly would run a daycare in her house for local working families. Shelly took it upon herself to teach the kids to read, do basic math, and follow schedules. In the sweltering heat of the summer months, she taught most of them how to swim in their large above-ground swimming pool. Teaching the children the academic basics and swimming was her idea. Shelly knew the parents were working hard for their children, and she took it upon herself to help them, but she could. It's what Shelly thought she should do, to run a day care. The parents appreciated her hard work and would thank her for bringing gifts at special times like Christmas. Shelly realized she didn't charge enough, but she did not mind. Shelly stays in contact with many parents and their children, who are now adults with their own children. She feels a bit like a grandma to the kids.

As the train sped through Central Wisconsin, Shelly realized she's hungry and did not know where the café car was. She asked the passenger. The passenger told her to walk upstairs and then back downstairs in another car. Shelly became lost going to the cafe, and went the wrong way. She became frustrated with for not being able to follow basic directions. She asked another passenger. He told her how to get there. She thanked the man.

Shelly arrived at the cafe car and saw there were vacant tables. She didn't want to risk having someone come and start up a conversation. Shelly wasn't in the mood. She would take the food to her seat. There were so many items to choose from that Shelly became confused and overwhelmed. Choosing the cheeseburger and chips, she walked back to the seat on the train after receiving the food. In her haste, Shelly forgot her drink. She got turned around after going back for it and forgot where to go. A slight panic set in and Shelly felt stupid, bewildered, and confused. Her seat was two cars away, but it seemed further. She managed to pull herself together enough to find a train employee.

"Excuse me. I don't know where my seat is. Can you help me find it?" Shelly asked.

"No problem. What is your seat number?"

After telling the employee her number, the woman led her back to her seat. Shelly reached into her purse to give her a tip. "No ma'am. I can't accept that. It was my pleasure to help you." Shelly sat down in her chair with her food as the woman left. She pulled out the little table attached to her chair on the side, set her plate on it, and ate the cheeseburger and chips.

Shelly finished up with her meal and tried to rest. Other than the sound of the wheels on the track, her train car was quiet. Shelly always thought more clearly when it was quiet. When alone in her apartment, it was silent. She had more ideas than she knew how to deal with, but she didn't have the tools or knowledge to deal with them. Shelly had thought back to why she was making this trip to her son's house in north Idaho. Gary and his wife Jessica, and Shelly's younger sister, Brooke James, live in north Idaho. Gary and Brooke had tried to persuade her to come out for a nice, long visit.

Shelly never enjoyed staying away from her own home for long periods. Whenever she visited her kids, she stayed away for never more than a week at a time. Shelly liked the comfort of her own place. Understandable, but she also didn't want to be a burden to her kids.

During the last phone call with Gary, Shelly told him of her hesitations about the trip. "I'm not really up to it. I just want to stay here."

"I understand, but I think you need to come out. Jessica said she would love to take care of you, and Aunt Brooke told me she wants to have you stay with her for a while."

"Gary, I guess you're right. I'll look at the times and cost for a train ticket," Shelly said with little enthusiasm.

On the train, Shelly still couldn't sleep. She thought back to her apartment and how she could be sitting in the brown recliner gazing out the window at the tall shrubs. There were some bird feeders outside the window. Cardinals and other birds fly from the shrubs to the feeder, gaining seeds each time before flying to the safety of the thick brush and branches.

Why did I leave? Shelly said to herself. Why am I even on this train? What was I thinking? I was comfortable and content in my chair inside my apartment. Shelly still couldn't get to sleep. Why didn't I bring my journal?

I need to write this stuff down on paper. Maybe it will help me.

Ten months ago, Shelly started a journal to write out her thoughts. Her daughter, Melanie, told her it might help deal with how she was feeling. As time went on, her depression had already gotten worse. Six months into the journal was especially telling:

June 23rd- Feeling so exhausted and depressed.

June 24th- Things have to get better. I need my family. Jesse visited me, but it just wasn't long enough. I'm so disappointed that my sister, Brooke, couldn't come out for a visit. I understand that she just wasn't able to make it. The kids are so busy with their own lives they don't have time for me. I don't want to go anywhere. Don't want to visit with people in my apartment complex. I don't enjoy playing the card games with them. Anymore, I want to lock my door and not come out. Perhaps I can just run away to some big city where no one knows me. My kids have money and could fly out for a few days to see me. Why don't they do that? It seems they never do. I really feel that I am slipping away fast, and no one cares.

June 26th- I don't want to go anywhere. Don't care for the people around me. I don't enjoy playing the cards. All they want to do is talk. I want to bury my head in the game. I want to stay inside and lock my door and never come out.

June 28th- I could run away and hide in some big city. My kids don't want me around. Liz and Kevin wouldn't even spend time with me the last time they visited. Gary and Jessica can't come out for a visit because of their kids and their large garden. Melanie is busy with work and family. Just yesterday, she told me she was going to the lake for lunch with her daughter. Why didn't they ask me to go?

June 29th- So, old age stinks. Golden years stink. I don't want to live to 90 or 100 like my grandmas and my aunts. I am ready for God to take me now.

June 30th- Why would my kids want to come see me? I live in a little apartment. There is nothing for them to do, but they can help me arrange my closets and shampoo my carpets for me. I get so confused with all my stuff and wish I could get rid of everything except one little room. I already got rid of a bunch of things after Jason passed away.

July 1st- I need to get rid of my stuff and go into assisted living. I don't want to go on. Maybe going to a nursing home will speed it up for me.

The last thought Shelly had before she fell asleep in Minnesota was Brooke's phone call in the middle of July, pleading with her to come out and visit Brooke in Idaho. Shelly recalled how Brooke sounded. Brooke must have sensed just how depressed Shelly had gotten. Both Brooke and Gary, urging her to go out to Idaho, convinced her to make the trip.

Soon after she thought about Brooke's call, she fell asleep with her small blanket over her and her neck nestled into the pillow. Shelly leaned against the window as the train passed through the Minnesota landscape during the night.

Late the next evening, around midnight, Shelly would be in Idaho. Little did she know that her life would soon take a turn for the better.

FLASHBACKS

In the morning, Shelly woke up groggy and stiff. Her seat in coach class was firm enough, but it wasn't great for sleeping. Shelly glanced out the window, trying to get her bearing, but only saw wheat fields. They must be somewhere in Minnesota or North Dakota.

Throat feeling dry, Shelly pulled water out from the bag and poured a refreshing drink. She reached for the small bag to find the toothbrush, toothpaste, and hairbrush. Then leaned over to check for a line to the restroom. Nobody was standing there.

The interior was small but bigger than airline bathrooms. It didn't appear too closed in, which helped give her space to breathe. As accommodating as the train was, she had a space to wash and brush. So Shelly began her morning bathroom ritual.

She started with fixing her hair. Shelly was never satisfied with how her hair looked. She sometimes made comments about how messy it was before anyone else could comment, nut they never did. Her kids and friends always say her hair looks fine—never out of place. Shelly looked again in the mirror. Dismayed by the tuft of hair that stuck up near her ear, she brushed her teeth. After finishing up in the bathroom, she returned to her seat.

Shelly had little appetite this morning, so she remained in her chair, opting for water and trail mix; the mix was something she always carried when traveling, no matter the distance. At lunchtime she will go to the cafe car.

The scenery appeared to stay the same. Farm fields with houses here and there. The stops at the stations were short. Stops in North Dakota and Montana were remote, with nothing much around them. Shelly couldn't understand how people could live in such remote places, especially with kids. She shook off the thought.

Since she'd left the Chicago station, Shelly had played no games on her laptop. Lisa, Shelly's granddaughter, loaded several games at her apartment. Lisa's brother, Nate, was supposed to load the game, but he had prior commitments. Shelly had every intention of playing them, but she wasn't up for any activity, including playing games on the computer. So she fell into her little routine of staring out the window or napping. One consolation was that Shelly would arrive late tonight in North Idaho.

There was plenty of time on the train and she thought again about her sister, Brooke, and her son, Gary, talking her into this trip. *Why did I let them talk me into this trip? I should have taken the plane instead.* Shelly doubted her decision to take the train, even though it had been a life-long goal for her. *So at least I'll be there late tonight.*

Lunchtime rolled around, and Shelly felt hungry. Unfortunately, the trail mix she had earlier only satisfied her for a few hours. Shelly walked to the cafe car and got a sandwich with chips. The sandwich was turkey and bacon, with Swiss cheese on flatbread and a cola as a treat. For Shelly, drinking soda was rare. Even in her younger days, she drank very little soda.

Back at her seat, Shelly dug into her food. The turkey and bacon sandwich wasn't great, but it was decent enough for being from a train cafe. After washing down the sandwich and chips with the cola, she settled into the routine she had to help pass the time.

Instead of staring out the window, she opened her laptop and played a few games of solitaire, which helped pass time quicker. Out the window, she noticed more hills in the landscape passing by her window. The rolling hills in Montana were getting larger. It was a good thing. When the hills grew into tall mountain peaks, it meant that Idaho was not far away.

Deep in her heart, Shelly knew this trip was good for her. So why was it so daunting? Her mind brought up thoughts from her past that plagued her for a while. Shelly thought of her kids and why they didn't spend more time visiting her.

Why didn't Liz and Kevin stay with me longer when they last visited me? Oh my god, they only stayed a few days. And they took the time to drive to Florida from California, saw a car race, and gave me two days. Don't they understand I'm old and most likely won't have much time left?

Thoughts racing through her mind switched to her youngest daughter, Melanie, and how they didn't visit very often, even though they live in the same small town. *Why doesn't Melanie or her kids stop in more often? I mean, she lives only a half-mile away from me. Would it kill them to stop in to see how I'm doing?*

Shelly's thoughts switched to her sister Brooke and how she could not drive from Minnesota when she visited her oldest son there. In her heart, she knew it would have been tough for Brooke to drive through Chicago at her age. Despite knowing she couldn't make the trip, it still hurt Shelly.

Brooke couldn't bother driving to see me earlier this year, when she was in Minnesota. I know she said at her age; it was hard and there weren't any routes that she could handle.

Back in her apartment, Shelly was watching an old show. Matlock with Andy Griffith was on TV. The episode was the rerun on a TV channel that played various shows from years ago.

It was the beginning of June of this same year. On the arm of the recliner, her water bottle was in the cup-holder. The side table was full of things such as books, magazines, and other knickknacks. Shelly didn't want to risk knocking over the water by setting it on the table.

While Shelly was watching the show, shutting out everything else, the phone had rung. It sat on the little side table next to her chair. Having it so close made it louder than usual. The sudden sound made her jump when the phone first rang. Shelly was easily frightened throughout her life. Someone coming in the room when she was not looking or a sudden sound, a telephone ringing, made her jump. Nobody was sure how it started. Maybe it was something from her childhood.

Shelly looked at the caller ID and saw it was Brooke.

"Hello, Brooke," Shelly was excited her sister called.

Shelly chats with Brooke often through the computer and talks to her on the phone. She was always happy to hear from her younger sister.

"I hope I'm not interrupting you."

"No. I was just watching Matlock." Shelly's racing heart calmed and slowed after hearing her sister's voice. reaching over to the TV remote, she muted the sound.

"The reason I'm calling is that CJ and I are driving out to Larry's and will spend time with him."

"Sounds like an enjoyable trip. Is CJ going to help with the driving?" Shelly asked, wondering how big CJ had gotten since she had last seen him. He must be fifteen years old now.

"CJ wants to drive the entire way. He's been doing well and drives a lot here in town." CJ is her great-grandson.

"That ought to help you a great deal. I know getting older makes it harder to drive longer distances." The thought of traveling anywhere came across to Shelly as daunting, but she was glad for her sister. Being able to see your family helps the soul, but many aging people get little opportunity because their kids may be living far away or because of financial strains.

"I thought that I'd want to drive down to visit you for four or five days. Would that be okay?"

Shelly's mood brightened. With a voice that could not contain her excitement at the idea, "Brooke, I'd love that!"

Shelly was excited about the idea of Brooke coming to see her. She would get to spend quality time with her sister. She began thinking of things for them to do while talking to Brooke.

"CJ and I are leaving in a week and a half and are getting things ready. Gary and Jessica said they would watch Jonah while we're gone."

Shelly thought of Jonah. Gary and Jessica loved to take in Brooke's schnauzer whenever she needed to leave town; its boundless energy and expressive face won their hearts at first sight. "Which way would you drive down here?"

"CJ and I are looking at routes tomorrow. I'll call you later and let you know."

"I can't wait." The promise in her sister's voice sounded like this trip that would actually happen.

"How about we talk more tomorrow or the next day? I have a lot of work to do to get ready for the trip, so we'll talk soon. Love you! Bye."

"Bye Brooke. Love you, too."

Shelly hung up the phone. Excitement bubbled up in her at the idea of Brooke coming for a visit. Throughout their lives, they never had much one-on-one time. Even as kids.

It had always been about the events and holidays when they'd gathered together in the past. There was always a need for attention or something to eat for the families. There was never time to sit and talk, but this will be a wonderful opportunity for quality time with Brooke. Shelly wanted to share what she had on her mind with Brooke and knew Brooke wanted to tell her things as well.

The next day came and went. No phone call from Brooke. Worry and doubt filled Shelly's mind, but she held on to the fact that Brooke would call and that they would have found a pleasant route by now.

The day after, the phone rang just before noon. Shelly saw it was her sister.

"Hi, Brooke," Shelly said with anticipation.

"It doesn't look like I'm going to get to drive down there from Larry's place in Minnesota."

"Couldn't find a good route?" Her stomach fell with

those words. Shelly couldn't help but feel disappointment, even if she didn't want to.

"No. CJ and I tried looking at different routes, and they all went through major cities or wound around way too far. Shelly, I really wanted to see you. There was the possibility of flying to Fort Wayne, but the nearest airport to Larry's house was four hours away. I feel so bad."

"I understand. Both of us are just getting too old to drive longer distances. Especially on our own."

"I know. I want to come see you, but I just can't make that trip on my own. If CJ were driving, it would be no problem," Brooke replied. "He is spending time with Larry, helping him with the construction jobs. Larry promised they'd go fishing, and CJ does not want to miss that."

"I'm going out to Gary and Jessica's in August. Let's visit then," Shelly tried to sound more positive.

"Shelly, I want to have at least two weeks with you to myself. Can we do that?"

Shelly was never comfortable staying anywhere for long. She could only handle a few days at a time, except with her kids.

"I don't know. Let's wait and see," Shelly said.

"I want you to stay for at least a month, but I can do two weeks. I want to cook for you so you won't have to do any work. We can have the quality time we have never had."

"I was only planning on staying a month on the entire trip, so I think I can do two weeks."

"So two weeks will be fine. I would love to have you stay with me longer, but two weeks will work. I think Gary and Jessica would be fine with that." Brooke replied.

"I'll talk to them and see. More than likely, they'd be okay with it. Maybe two weeks there and two weeks with you," Shelly decided. That sounded good.

"I like that and I know Gary will be fine with it. You know he and Jessica want the best for you and are pretty easygoing about stuff like this. Oh Shelly! It's going to be good. After Mark moved out, I turned his old den into a little office with a bed. I'll get that ready for you," Brooke said excitedly.

"Let's make this happen." Shelly could feel this was going to happen.

She felt that her little sister needed to talk after they hung up. They'd never really spoken of their childhoods to each other before. Shelly had things she wanted to discuss with Brooke as well.

Despite Shelly being able to visit with her sister soon, it still hurt her about Brooke not being able to drive to her place.

At least I'll see her in Idaho, but I still don't understand why she couldn't drive here to see me. I wanted to show off my little apartment and the friends I made. I wanted her to see Melanie and her family.

There I go. Feeling sorry for myself again. Snap out of it, Shelly. She thought to herself.

Shelly had to get herself together. She was seeing

Gary and Jessica late tonight. She opened her little bag and got a handful of cheese and crackers that a friend from her apartment had given her for the trip. They are coming in handy now. Not to satisfy the hunger, but as a diversion to get her mind off the depressing thoughts she was having.

A walk to the observation deck would let me stretch out my legs. After eating pieces of cheese and crackers, Shelly walked up to the observation deck in another train car. Since it was on the upper deck, she got a brief workout walking up those stairs. It was a chance to stretch her legs. Not bad for 82 years old, she thought.

The observation car was full of people talking amongst themselves. Shelly had hoped to get a seat to herself, but the only open seats available were among groups. She didn't want to visit with anyone. All she could do was walk through the car and return to her chair—her small home during this trip.

Soon the call for the dining car and the cafe car sounded. Shelly wasn't that hungry. She walked upstairs to the cafe for a bag of potato chips and a cup of coffee. There were strips of beef jerky in her bag she ate with the chips.

Not much longer now! Thank God! Shelly thought.

The sun was getting lower in the sky. She could see they were nearing Glacier National Park. Shelly could still see the mountains before it became too dark. The West Glacier train stop was the longest stop in a while. It was a big destination landmark for travelers and hikers going to the Park for the magnificent scenery. It was understandable, so the delay didn't bother her. She stayed seated, not wanting to impede people getting on and off the train.

As the train left West Glacier, Montana, Shelly's thoughts drifted again. The thoughts drifted to her recent past, centered on the day her second husband, Jason Murphy, died from his six-month battle with cancer.

It was in May 2018. Hospice was at the apartment and told Shelly that today was the day Jason would most likely succumb to the cancer. He had eaten nothing in two weeks. Jason could not hold down the water. His daughters from his first marriage were there: Connie and Tina. Melanie was there as well. The daughters lived near them at the time in northern Indiana, and Shelly was grateful for that. She didn't know what she would have done without the girls. Shelly knew Jason was happier having them by his side at the end.

Jason laid on his favorite recliner, covered in the old brown blanket he had used to cover up with during the many winters in past years. His mom gave him the blanket when he was young.

The hospice worker monitored Jason, checking his breathing and pulse. She let Shelly and the daughters know Jason was nearing his end and to prepare. Stubborn as ever, he was still hanging on and refused to pass.

Throughout the day, Melanie had trouble dealing with her dad's imminent death. She sat on the bed, not able to handle what was happening in the living room.

As horrible as it sounded, Jason's holding on had only been prolonging the emotional pain they were all feeling. Shelly went back to console Melanie, but it did little to soothe her pain, so they used the moment to share their sorrow.

Connie and Tina remained at their father's side, sitting with him and hoping he knew they were there. "Dad! Connie and I are here. It's okay to let go." Connie looked at Tina, then back at her dad, "You don't need to suffer anymore."

Shelly and Melanie walked into the living room to join them. "How are you doing, Melanie?" asked Tina. "A little better. How is dad doing now?" trying to stifle the tears.

Attempting to hold back the tears and be strong for everyone, she could not keep it together. Tears were flowing down the side of her cheeks and dropping onto her shirt. She used a tissue to wipe them and her nose.

Connie told Melanie that their dad was still hanging on to what brief life he had left. "He's stubborn right up to the end." That brought a small, half-hearted chuckle from the women.

An idea struck Tina. She wasn't sure it would work, but didn't want him suffering anymore. She walked to the little bookcase and grabbed a flashlight and a small porcelain angel. "Take the angel. Let's see if we can help Dad let go." Tina turned on the flashlight and pointed it at Jason. "Connie, hold up the angel. Dad? Can you hear me? Follow the angel into the light. Tina said this as she waved the flashlight around Jason's line of sight. It was silly, but she was willing to try anything. "Come on, Dad, help us. It's time to let go and stop the suffering." Tina and Connie kept waving the flashlight and angel around, attempting to prompt Jason to die in peace.

Melanie joined in to encourage her dad to let go. Shelly sat on the sofa opposite the recliner that Jason was in, not wanting to interfere. The apartment was small. Having the three daughters and the hospice worker around Jason made things tight.

While coaxing her dad to pass, Melanie broke down again and ran back into the bedroom. Shelly went after her and asked, "Melanie, are you okay? What can I do?" "Nothing Mom. It's... It's just hard. I don't want him to suffer, but I don't want him to leave," using a tissue to help with her tears.

A few minutes later, the phone rang. It was Gary. Connie answered the phone. "How is Jason doing? How are you all doing?" He asked. "It's rough, but he is being his old stubborn self," she chuckled a bit. "We've been trying to coax him to pass on by holding up a flashlight and an angel telling him to go into the light." She noticed the hospice worker saying something and had to pause. "Wait, something's happening," Connie said. "Oh, my god, it's happening," Gary told her to hang up and go to Jason, and he hung up the phone. Connie and Tina shouted for Shelly and Melanie. The hospice worker confirmed it would be any second now.

Shelly and Melanie ran into the living room. "Shelly,

Dad's nearly gone," Tina said. Tracks of tears trickled down all their faces. Besides Melanie, there had been no crying until now. They had been expecting this for a while. But now that it was happening, none of them could keep from crying.

A few moments later, the hospice nurse spoke. "He's gone. I'll call the Veteran's Administration now so they can come and take care of him." Jason had served in the Navy when he was young. It was comforting to know that they were handling his cremation.

When the Veteran's representatives arrived, they asked the women to go to the bedroom while they worked. They gathered in the bedroom, but said little. Melanie sat on the bed, crying, while Shelly sat beside her with her arm around her, comforting her daughter.

Tina and Connie sat in the two small chairs near the bed. It saddened them, but neither of them was crying now. They didn't have to wait long. A Veteran's representative walked to the bedroom to inform them they had finished and Jason was ready for viewing.

When they walked into the living room, they saw Jason on the gurney, lying with his arms folded across his chest. Jason had a white sash wrapped around his head for display. He had an American flag covering him. Shelly commented she was thankful the representatives took the time to do this for her husband. Melanie's tears were drying up after crying. She seemed more calm now that she saw her dad looking peaceful.

After viewing Jason on the gurney in the living room,

the representatives suggested it was time to wheel him outside into the night. They asked the family to proceed out first. The Hurst waited just outside the apartment in the driveway. The Veteran's reps wheeled the gurney out, adhering to strict ceremony and maintaining perfect steps as they moved to the waiting Hurst.

Two men stood on one side, and two stood on the other. They folded the flag, and once done, one man presented the folded flag to Shelly. She accepted it and thanked him. In unison, the representatives moved the gurney into the Hurst. Shelly and the daughters thanked the representatives for the care and professionalism they showed Jason.

Shelly felt a hand shaking her forearm, which startled her. She looked up and saw the train conductor standing by her. "We'll be stopping in Sandpoint in twenty minutes." It was around one in the morning.

On the train, the conductors write each passenger's stop on a piece of paper that is placed above them. It is a simple method of knowing who gets off at what stops. Especially for stops in the middle of the night when most people sleep.

Trying to shake off the sleep, Shelly gathered her things and packed them away. About a minute later, her cell phone rang. She looked at who was calling out of habit, but Shelly was sure it was Gary.

"Hi, Gary. Are you at the station now?" Asked Shelly.

"Mom, it's Jessica. We're still on the road and might be late. Close to Sandpoint, we got stuck behind road construction. It's been ten minutes so far, and I don't know how much longer we'll be."

"Well, that's alright. If I get to the station before you do, I'll just wait there until you guys arrive."

"Okay mom. We wanted to be there when you got off the train, but I'm not sure if we can make it on time. We'll try to get there as soon as possible. Oh! By the way, Rylie's here with us," Jessica said.

"That's great! I can't wait to see you guys," Shelly said. It was late, but she did not mind waiting. It will give her time to breathe in the fresh Idaho summer air she hasn't breathed in for a long time.

"Bye, Mom."

"Bye, Jessica."

Shelly hung up and finished getting her stuff ready. Since it was dark outside, she couldn't see too much, but she knew she was a few minutes from Sandpoint. Ahead, the night sky from her window was, to a degree, brighter thanks to the street lights within and around the town of Sandpoint.

Shelly felt more relieved than excited while the train slowed. It was a long trip. She was considering returning her train ticket to Indiana and getting a plane ticket instead. Maybe I'll wait a little while. I'll decide in a week or two.

As it neared the old train station in Sandpoint, the train slowed down. The front cars of the train stopped at the platform first. The station's platform was small, so she had to wait about five minutes for the train to pull forward for her car.

Shelly had her bags together, waiting for the train to come to a complete stop. Once it stopped, she got up from the seat she had called home for the last couple of days and headed for the door.

The train door opened, and Shelly stepped out of the train car into the fresh, early morning Idaho air.

Only a few people got off the train. The platform was mostly empty.

ARRIVING IN IDAHO

Shelly felt the chilly crispness in the air stepping off the train late in the evening, or very early in the morning in Sandpoint, Idaho. Forgetting just how cool north Idaho gets at night in the summer, even at the end of August. Glad for having brought her sweatshirt, she also noticed how crisp the air was. The weather in Indiana is much more humid, and the nighttime temperatures do not drop like it does in north Idaho.

Shelly walked down the short platform and ran across a conductor. He had been making sure things ran on time on the train. "Hello, Ma'am. If your ride isn't here yet, you can wait inside the station. The interior may be small, but it's warm in there."

"Thank you. I'll do that."

Once inside the old building, she sat down on one of the wooden benches and started watching the window for Gary and Jessica. By then, most people who got off the train already departed, and she was alone in the terminal.

Shelly stayed inside the station for only a few minutes, but decided it was too stuffy indoors and wanted to breathe in that fresh air. Wheeling her suitcase with her purse and blanket stacked on top, she took a slow, deliberate breath and then exhaled to calm herself. Despite the blaring lights of the train station, the night sky was so clear. The stars were brighter than she remembered. The breeze picked up, danced through the surrounding pine trees, and wove through her hair, messing it up a bit. *Oh! My hair. It must look like a mess now.* After brushing it down, she found a spot next to the station to sit and wait.

Gary and Jessica were on their way, but delayed by the road construction. She wanted them to be there when she arrived. Shelly wasn't concerned about being alone like that in the early morning. She knew there was low crime up there and that people were pretty friendly.

Shelly had time to think about her son. About how guilty she felt about having him and Jessica drive up this late at night while watching the small street leading up to the station. No matter how many times they insisted, she still felt guilty.

Shelly thought about how Gary struggled through rough times in the 1990s over 25 years ago. Shelly never realized how much he struggled. Gary didn't talk to her about it, so she assumed everything was okay. About a year back, he confided in her about his financial issues. Gary struggled to find jobs that paid him enough to live on, and sometimes he had very little to eat. Since Shelly and Jason lived about half an hour away from Gary in the early nineties, he would show up occasionally for a visit. He did this when he had little food in his cupboard and would have dinner with them. I don't blame him.

Gary struggled in college, but he made it through. However, the financial burden of the tuition was substantial for him and put him in more debt than he would have liked. He had lived in her and Jason's basement in Indiana for a time after her and Jason moved back there from Idaho, trying to find jobs, but she never saw him give up. Shelly recalls seeing him constantly sending out resumes and never getting replies. Shelly remembered how he sent applications for positions he was qualified for, but got no callbacks. She felt horrible for him. Shelly could not understand why he couldn't get hired anywhere, especially since Gary had experience from the military and a bachelor's degree.

As he told her about this time in his life, her heart ached for him. She wished she could have done more. Gary assured her it was okay, and that Shelly had helped him more than she realized.

When Gary thought there was no hope, he found a good job. Shelly was excited to see things turn around for him, however, she didn't realize how life-changing it would be. During this time, Gary met Jessica, who was perfect for him. Shelly thought back with fond memories of how quickly she and her daughter-in-law had bonded.

Gary has been in a great place for years, both financially and family-wise. He has a fantastic wife and two brilliant and polite kids. Shelly hadn't had to worry about him in quite a while. Not any more than parents would worry about their kids, no matter their age.

Shelly saw a car's headlights approach up the small side street and knew it had to be them. She couldn't see inside the car, but was sure it was theirs. Gary flashed his high beams off and on and Shelly knew it was them.

The morning after, light streamed through the curtains, and Shelly woke up on the futon in Gary and Jessica's office/den. Despite its tacky, old Caribbean island print, it was surprisingly comfortable. Jessica had set up a little folding table as a nightstand, where Shelly had put her hearing aids and her small laptop computer before going to sleep. Shelly ended up sleeping later than usual at home. The train trip and getting in late at the station tired her.

When she reached for the hearing aids, she saw a steaming cup of coffee and a little plate of cheese and crackers. *That Jessica, bless her heart. She didn't have to do this.* Shelly thought while smiling. She sat on the edge of the bed and ate the food on the platter, then washed it down with the coffee.

With the plate and mug in hand, she walked upstairs

while trying to fully wake up. Jessica was in the kitchen, putting away dishes.

"Good morning, Mom," Jessica said. "How did you sleep?"

"Pretty good. That futon was comfy. I woke up and saw the plate of crackers and coffee on the table. Jessica, you didn't have to go through the trouble." Shelly slept well enough, but since she hadn't spent the night in her own bed, she didn't sleep as well as she could have.

"It was no trouble, Mom. You had a long trip, and you deserved a good night's sleep."

Shelly sat down at the dining table with her coffee cup. Jessica saw her cup was empty. "Would you like more coffee, Mom?"

"Please!"

Jessica got a cup for herself, took the pot to the table, poured her another cup, poured herself a cup, and sat down.

"I'm so glad you're here with us, Mom," giving Shelly a warm smile.

"It's good to be here," Shelly said, feeling cold. "I forgot how chilly it gets in the morning. I'm glad I wore my sweater."

Later, Gary walked into the dining room. "Good morning, sleepy head."

"Morning," Gary said with a slight smile. He was still groggy from the late night. His hair matted on the side and back of his head.

Gary walked up to Jessica, hugged her, and then gave

her a kiss on the cheek. "Good morning, my love." He had not brushed his teeth yet, having just woken up, and wanted to spare her his morning breath.

"Good morning, honey. Want some breakfast?"

"Not right now. I'll wait. So, mom, what do you want to do today?"

"You know, even though I've been sitting on the train for the past couple of days, I kind of just want to relax," Shelly said.

"Okay. It sounds good and believe me. I understand," grabbing a glass of water for himself.

As they all settled into the dining room at the kitchen table, Gary and Jessica's nineteen-year-old daughter, Rylie, came out from her room.

As she joined them in the dining room, they exchanged morning greetings. When Rylie sat down, they all heard their son, Jeff, come upstairs. He hadn't seen his Grandma Shelly since Gary and Jessica brought her from the train station late last night.

Jeff is fifteen years old and goes to the local high school. He plays on the high school football team and works at the same supermarket Rylie works at.

Jeff walked over and gave his grandma a big hug. It had been a couple of years since Shelly had seen him.

"My goodness. You have grown so much!"

"I hope I grow more. I'm already taller than dad," Jeff said.

Gary laughed as he shook his head in agreement. After talking about the kids for a bit, Shelly talked about the people in her apartment building and how she just wanted to stay inside and lock the door. The recent change in her attitude and her depressive state concerned Gary, Jessica, and the rest of Shelly's kids, each of whom expressed their concerns to one another.

Jessica had changed the subject a bit. It helped bring Shelly out of her current depression spell. Just being at Gary and Jessica's house has already helped her. She was cheering up. Getting away from the things that were making her depressed, or at least contributing, helped provide Shelly some relief.

Later on, downstairs in the living room, when Shelly and Rylie spent some time together, they got onto the subject of their family tree. It was a subject that Rylie had a keen interest in. She had already found some information on an ancestry website and wanted to share her findings and put stories behind the names of the family.

There were two particular findings Rylie wanted to share, so she started with the more general one first. "Grandma! I've been looking through an ancestor site. I found at least six of our family names on both the mothers and fathers sides of our family. They trace back to America before the founding of the United States. Most of the ancestors came through the northeast and originated from England, Wales, Ireland, and Scotland. One line came from Germany."

"I didn't know that. Never would I have guessed we had any German in us." Shelly saw how fascinated her granddaughter was by this. She knew little about the family besides close relatives, most of whom died before she was old enough to know them.

"Well, there's no German heritage on your side of the family. But you've got the other nationalities that I was talking about. It was dad's Grandma Jorgensen's side of the family way back, who had ancestors from Germany," Rylie said. "And the other thing. Your grandpa on your mom's side has pictures here. I was wondering if you had already seen them."

Shelly had never seen the first photograph before. It was her grandfather as a little boy, looking rather serious beside his sister, who appeared equally stony-faced and serious. The second photo was more familiar to her. It was a small photoshoot of her grandparents and their son and daughters. They were dressed in their Sunday best and stood in front of the curtains in the living room. Shelly saw her mom in the photograph. She had a rare smile and looked beautiful in the photo.

"Can you send these pictures to me?"

"Of course. I could probably send it to dad first so he can make them look better."

"Thank you, Rylie. I love having a brilliant granddaughter," Shelly said as she hugged her.

The family spent the rest of the week visiting each other, going out to eat, and just spending time together. Something that she will get to do with her sister, Brooke. Shelly doesn't remember ever getting to spend quality one-on-one time with Brooke.

She is about seven years older than her, and they had spent a lot of time apart during their childhood. Throughout their adult lives, the times they could spend with each other were with their kids and their husbands around. They never talked in depth about their past. Both of them were hoping to talk about it this time.

With both of their husbands gone, Brooke's through divorce, and Shelly losing her second husband to cancer, the only distraction they would have was Brooke's dog, Jonah. Jonah is a cute Schnauzer whose eyes could melt the hearts of the toughest men. He always welcomed visitors by barking until they petted him.

Jonah would especially go nuts whenever Gary and Jessica dropped by for a visit. They watched him when Brooke had to go some place for an extended trip and couldn't take Jonah with her.

The week at Gary and Jessica's went by fast. It was time for Shelly to go to Brooke's for some much-needed quality time. Gary told Brooke they could drive her there, but she wanted to pick Shelly up. She had planned to take her to lunch before driving to her place.

Shelly had packed her suitcase, but left some of her things at Gary's house. She didn't need to take everything. They waited in the living room, watching out the big window.

"This is going to do you a world of good. You and Aunt Brooke never really had much time together without people around," Gary said.

"I know. I'm not sure what to expect. Are we able to

visit each other for that entire time? Am I going to be bored? Am I going to bore her? Are we going to cry a lot? I just don't know. She said she wants to cook for me, too. I just hope I won't be too much trouble."

"Aunt Brooke is happy to have you stay over. Just think of her as the doting little sister," Gary said.

Rylie saw from the window that Brooke had pulled up outside. They went to the door to welcome her inside. Brooke gave her big sister a long hug. She also hugged the other family members.

"Shelly, I am so glad you're here. I have some plans for us starting tomorrow morning, but today we will just have lunch and then go home and relax. How does that sound?" Brooke said.

"Sounds good. Just tell me what we are doing before it happens. I'm game for anything. Well, anything that these 82-year-old bones can do."

Shelly and Brooke headed outside to her car, and Gary and Jessica followed them with her suitcase in hand.

They said their goodbyes, and then Brooke and Shelly drove off.

BROOKE'S PLACE

When the two sisters arrived at Brooke's house, they spent the rest of the day sharing news about recent events in each other's lives. Brooke told Shelly about the divorce from Mark, how life was for her in retirement. Brooke was a workaholic, so the transition to retirement needed some time to adjust.

Shelly talked about life at the apartment and the friends who help her. Especially one woman, a fair amount younger than Shelly, who drives her wherever she needs to go.

"Brooke, I love where I live, but I'm often overwhelmed. Many other residents stop by to visit when all I would like to do is rest. I don't turn them away, I just sit there and listen because I don't want to hurt any feelings. Sometimes, someone else knocks on the door while visiting with someone else."

"I'd assume that the attention would be nice, but I can see your point about it happening all the time," Brooke said.

"The one woman I told you about who drives me places is very nice, but we have very different political views. We talk about everything but politics. Besides, I don't want to lose a good friend and a reliable ride." Both Shelly and Brooke chuckled.

They were ready for a good night's sleep as the evening wore on. Brooke wanted Shelly to rest for the next day. As long as Shelly was here, she needed to cover a lot of things. Brooke knew her sister was having problems with depression. There were a lot of things she needed to cover while Shelly was there. Brooke knew her sister was having problems with depression. The church program she was using herself helped her a great deal. It took much longer than what Brooke would spend with her big sister. She'd take whatever time she had and hope it was enough to bring Shelly out of the dangerous part of her depression.

After getting a good night's sleep, Brooke fixed some breakfast. She wanted to make something special for Shelly her first morning there.

Brooke got a couple of small plates and arranged a sliced avocado, a boiled egg, some wedges of nectarines, and some English muffins on the plates. Brooke was satisfied with how the food looked.

"Breakfast is ready." Brooke walked out with the plate and a glass of orange juice. She set the breakfast down on a little TV tray by Shelly.

"Oh, my goodness. Brooke, you didn't have to go through the trouble. The food looks so nice," Shelly said.

"No problem at all. I'll go get mine, and we can relax," Brooke replied, happy with Shelly's reaction to the care she took in fixing breakfast.

After they finished eating and Brooke cleaned up, she walked to the living room and sat at the end of the sofa. Jonah jumped up and laid down beside her, resting his eyes.

Shelly sat in the recliner near the sofa, relaxing with Brooke. The breakfast was satisfying. In the past, when she spent time with her sister, there were always other family members needing their attention. The conversations they had centered on husbands, kids, or grandkids and never on themselves.

"When we talked last night, I mentioned something about the people at the apartment complex. I forgot to add one thing that's been weighing on me."

"What is it?" Brooke asked, wondering what it was.

"Some people in the complex meet in the rec room and start talking about God and the Bible or how they relate to us. I couldn't contribute anything to the conversation. I can't seem to recall any of the verses," Shelly commented.

"Shelly, don't feel bad about that. A lot of people have trouble remembering them." Brook reassured her.

"I know," Shelly replied. She raised her arms up to her chest, balled up her hands under her face, and said, "I just can't remember any of the Bible verses. I must be stupid because of it. The other ladies at the apartment must think I'm dumb."

"Now stop that, Shelly," Brooke snapped at her. Brooke did not like Shelly talking about herself like that. "Shelly, you are not dumb. From what you say, the ladies in the apartment complex don't think you're dumb."

"It just seems that way when I can't recall the verses," replied Shelly. "Well, I guess I'm not a very good Christian."

Brooke tried to comfort her big sister. The way Shelly had answered and the way she held her hands and shook worried Brooke. *Could she have dementia?* Brooke contemplated. It didn't run in their family. Shelly was still shaking a bit. Brooke had to calm her down. She had to reassure Shelly again that she was not stupid.

"Just because you can't recite Bible verses from memory doesn't mean you're not a good Christian. To apply it and find the passage and meaning is more important." Brooke said. Her voice constricted, but she tried to sound as comforting as she could to Shelly.

Shelly sighed, "I guess you're right," still not convinced.

"You've seen my Bible. It's marked up and has little sticky notes all over it. I can't remember many verses, but I sure know where they are. I can go right to them to read when I need to," exclaimed Brooke.

"Thanks, Brooke. I needed that." Shelly brightened up after hearing that. She thought it would be a good idea to write things out and make notes. Shelly had trouble with short-term memory. Two of her kids and at least one of her grandkids also had problems with short-term memory; but they have always had excellent long-term memory recall. Gary, her son, often jokes that he thinks of something to say or look up on the computer, and when he gets upstairs or to the computer, he forgets. But ask him something that happened several years ago and he can tell you every detail

"Glad I could help," Brooke said. "Now, let's get on to what I had wanted to share with you before I forget," Brooke told Shelly. They both shared a laugh.

Brooke began, "About two years ago, I went with Mark to a 12-step meeting. Do you recall when I told you he was having trouble with alcohol? Well, I attended the meeting to support him. As we walked into the building, I saw that other counseling meetings were going on. I was curious, so I looked through them and saw one that caught my eye. I don't know why it did, but it drew me to it. It was a group meeting for co-dependency."

"Really?" Shelly said. It surprised her that Brooke would want to go to a meeting focusing on co-dependency. Shelly always saw her as very independent. Brooke was always successful in the jobs she had and had gotten promotions. "That sounds like something you wouldn't have needed. I mean, you have always been pretty independent."

"That's what I assumed at first. It was like something was pushing me towards the room. I bet it was God's way of getting me in there." Brooke replied.

Brooke continued, "Once the meeting started, I found out pretty soon that co-dependency wasn't what I thought it was."

Just then, Jonah got up and gave Brooke the look. He needed to go outside to take care of business. Brooke excused herself and let Jonah out into the small backyard. She came back, sat down, and continued where she left off prior to taking care of Jonah.

"Co-dependency is about trying to control things I shouldn't try to control, focusing on other people and their actions more than myself. Since I'm a workaholic, I started to see that it wasn't so much about Mark as it was about me not seeing things the way they were," Brooke explained.

"I'm not sure I understand. Can you give me an example?" Shelly prompted.

Brooke continued, "One thing the meeting touched on was controlling others, but in the way I never imagined."

"What was that?" Shelly asked.

"One example was making suggestions to people, such as when someone's own kids would do something, they'd see it and suggest another way to do it," Brooke said.

"I do that all the time," Shelly stated. "I was always

just wanting to help." She thought back to all the times she did this to the kids and had a sudden attack of guilt.

"Turns out I wasn't helping them, but I was making them feel like nothing they did was right," Brooke responded. She saw from Shelly's reaction that she recognized the same thing that she had done to her kids in past years.

Shelly began telling Brooke about her youngest daughter, Melanie. "Melanie told me about several times she never felt she could do anything right. She said I was always trying to get her to do things a different way or suggesting other ways to do something. I thought I was making suggestions to help and didn't listen to her. I assumed she was just being difficult," Shelly said, tearing up from the thought. "Come to think of it, Gary has told me that a few times as well." Shelly was crying now as she realized what she had done to her kids. "I must have been a horrible mother," she said while crying.

Brooke tried to comfort her. "Shelly, I did the same thing. Whenever C.J. stays over, he says, I do it to him, and it makes him feel bad, like he can't do anything right." Brooke grabbed a tissue. These flaws were difficult to confront.

"All this time, I imagined I was helping them. Didn't know I was doing this to them," Shelly said as she wiped the tears from her eyes. The realization hurt her, shaking her head in disbelief.

"At least you're realizing it now. That's a tremendous step, Shelly. From what I've learned about these things, to help fix the problem, you need to discover where the problem came from to begin to heal. Then you try to recognize the times when you did this. That's when we can correct it."

"Do you think it'll help me? I've had so much happen to me throughout my life. Stevie dying, what happened to mom, watching dad and Jason die of cancer, and what Bill did to me and how that ended. I don't think I can get over it," Shelly said as she still cried.

"Shelly, look at me. I promise you we are going to get through this, and you will be much better. Look at how far I've come in just these past two years," Brooke said.

Brooke saw the pain in her face and eyes. She recognized that same pain in herself when she first recognized her own problems and where they had originated.

Shelly sniffed and wiped her nose with a tissue. "I hope we can, but I'm afraid I'm just too far gone."

"I will not accept that, Shelly," Brooke said. "Not accept it at all. We have a lot of steps to go through, but for now, we should focus on co-dependency."

Shelly sat up straighter in the recliner. She toughened her resolve by wiping her nose again with the tissue. "Ok, I'm ready," she declared. "Let's do this."

THE STORIES BEGIN

Brooke began. "The first thing that hit me when I learned of co-dependency was when Larry and his wife divorced. Larry's wife left him with four little kids to raise. I didn't want to involve myself with it, so I focused on work. I tried working overtime hours whenever possible." Brooke started crying. "Guilt stayed with me, even now, but I'm trying to accept what happened and learn from it."

Shelly replied, "Look at everything you have done for those grandkids since then. Brooke, you have more than made up for the past mistakes. You know I'm right about this."

"Yes, I guess so. I've come so far, Shelly, but I have trouble with that part of my past. I've tried to come to terms and get over it, but I still struggle, believe me. I am making good progress with it, though."

Shelly began talking about her past and the things she regretted. She hoped that by changing the topic to herself, it may help her little sister.

"I was controlling when it came to making suggestions. From what you told me about it, I can see it now. When Bill was alive, I didn't stand up to him and protect the kids as I should have, especially Jesse," Shelly said, now tearing up more.

Brooke brought over another box of tissues to break the tension. "I might need to go buy more tissue. We're sure going to need them. There are wads of tissue in the garbage can beside us."

That brought a pleasant smile from Shelly as she grabbed another tissue and wiped her eyes. "Yes, we definitely need more of them."

"Anyway, there was one time when Jesse was in little league baseball. Bill kept yelling at him during one game, telling Jesse he was doing things wrong. Bill was embarrassing Jesse and myself, but I didn't stop him." If I tried to prevent him, or intervene in any way, I feared what he might do to me and the kids. "

"Given Bill's history and the things he did to you, I certainly can understand."

Shelly continued, still sobbing and getting choked up somewhat. "Well, when we got home, Bill was still yelling at him. When we walked into the living room, he picked up Jesse and threw him across the room."

"That's terrible, Shelly," Brooke said with her eyes wide.

"Jesse landed on his side, and I could see it might have hurt him. He got up and just stood there and started crying but trying not to at the same time. I don't think he wanted to anger Bill any more than he already was."

Brooke shook her head in disbelief and expressed her sympathy.

Shelly continued, "But the worst part of it was that I just stood there. I didn't yell at Bill to stop, and even worse, I didn't see if Jesse was okay afterward. I just walked into the kitchen as if it had never happened." Shelly was crying more after this story. "Jesse must've thought I was terrible for not checking on him. But Brooke, I was afraid of what Bill might've done to me or to Jesse if I did go check on him."

Brooke wanted to console her sister. To say the right thing and was not sure what she could say. It broke her heart to see Shelly sad.

"Shelly, you were very young. It's not like you had a good role model for this kind of thing. Mom wasn't the comforting mother type, but you are. Remember that you were most likely afraid of what Bill would do if you had gone to Jesse to see if he was okay or not."

Just hearing that improved Shelly's mood. "Yes. I guess you're right, but it's still hard to handle the guilt."

At that point, Brooke decided it was a good time for a break. Both ladies getting hungry, so she walked into the kitchen to fix lunch.

While Brooke was in the kitchen, she quietly got out the phone and texted her niece, Liz.

Brooke: Hi Liz, Aunt Brook here. Your mom's with me and I wish you could be here. She needs you, so please try to come.

Liz: Wish I could but super busy with the kids and grandkids. Going to a wedding soon, sorry.

Brooke: I understand. Bye.

Liz: Bye.

Brooke understood why Liz could not make the trip. She knew Liz and Kevin had busy lives since they retired.

Brooke fixed herself and Shelly a serving of chicken Alfredo with parmesan and breadsticks. It was easy to prepare, and she had most of it prepared ahead of time. She likes to fix meals ahead of time in large amounts and save them for later. It has saved her a great deal of time overall.

When she took the plates into the living room for the two of them, Shelly's cell phone rang with one of the common ring tones. Shelly saw it was Gary calling.

"Hi mom. Are you and aunt Brooke going to be home today or tomorrow?" Gary asked.

"Yes, we're not going anywhere. Why do you ask?"

"I'm going into town later today or maybe tomorrow, and I might stop by," Gary answered.

"Is Jessica coming along, too?"

"No, only me. I'm doing something in town and wanted to drop by for a quick visit."

"Alright! I'll see you when you get here," Shelly replied.

"Sounds good. Bye, mom."

"Bye."

After hanging up the phone, she told Brooke about Gary coming over later today or tomorrow. Shelly continued to eat after she finished speaking on the cell phone with Gary. Brooke had been eating throughout their brief phone conversation and was nearly finished.

"This pasta and the breadsticks are delicious, Brooke. Are these the same breadsticks that Gary makes?"

"They sure are, and they were easier to fix than I first imagined. Gary told me I could make up a double batch, bake them halfway, and freeze them. Then whenever I need breadsticks for a meal, I can just brown them in my air fryer, and they'll stay fresh much longer," Brooke explained.

"How do you like your air fryer?" Shelly asked. "I have a small one, and I seem to use it more than my microwave."

Brooke replied, "I love it, and I'm using it as much as the microwave. I like the way it heats leftovers like pizza or cooks garlic bread." Shelly nodded in agreement.

After lunch, the emotions had settled to a comfortable level, and the tears dried. Brooke gathered the plates and cups and took them into the kitchen. She rinsed off the dishes with a small stream of water from the faucet and set the dishes in the sink. She will take care of them later.

"I have to run some errands, and I bet we need the break. Wanna ride along with me?" Brooke asked.

"Sure! I could use a day out. It'd be fun," Shelly replied, content with staying inside, but did not pass up the chance to get out for a drive. She was not interested in seeing the town. Shelly and Jason had lived in the region over thirty years ago. So she has seen everything she wanted to in north Idaho in the past.

"Good. I'll text Gary and let him know we won't be home for a while. He can swing by tomorrow, Brooke said.

Brooke and Shelly cleaned up and left for the afternoon.

The ladies did not get back until late in the day. Brooke decided that before they resumed their talks of their past, she would fix dinner for them.

"I was thinking of fixing chicken enchiladas and a salad. How does that sound?" asked Brooke.

"Sounds good. But you don't need to go to the trouble. Something simple is fine with me," Shelly replied. To her, Brooke was going through too much trouble just for her.

"It's no trouble. I already have the chicken separated and the can of enchilada sauce. It'll be a piece of cake," Brooke stated. She was glad to dote on her big sister.

"Ok. Can I help? I'm sure there's something I can do."

"Don't worry, I've got this, Shelly. You just get settled in, and I'll call you when it's ready. We're going to eat at the dining table. Is that okay?"

"Of course it is. I'd probably end up spilling some

sauce on my shirt if I were to hold the plate while sitting in the recliner." Shelly said as she chuckled.

Shelly and Brooke finished eating, and Brooke took care of the dishes. Both of the women grabbed a cup of coffee, sat down in the living room again, and resumed where they had left off before the meal.

Jonah hopped up on the sofa and snuggled beside Brooke, taking his rightful place by her side.

Shelly started, "Now, where were we?"

"You were telling me about Jesse." Brooke answered.

"Right! Well, there was another time when we were traveling someplace back in the Midwest. I don't recollect where it was. The kids were in the back seat. They were little at the time. Jesse must have done something that Bill didn't like. He reached into the backseat while driving, grabbed Jesse's hair, pulled him right up against the seat, and put him in a headlock. We were on a bridge, and he lost control of the car a little. The car swerved to the side towards the edge. It looked as if we were going to drive right off the bridge."

"What did you do?" Brooke asked.

"I grabbed at the wheel to get control. Jesse was screaming. Bill hit him a few times while he had him by the head. Liz and Gary were screaming for him to stop. It seemed like it lasted forever, but I'm sure it was less than a minute now that I look back," Shelly stated.

"I never consoled him or saw if he was okay later on after the incident. I just carried on as if it never happened," said Shelly.

Tears began welling up again in her eyes. Shelly still carried the guilt for all the times she didn't comfort and protect Jesse. "Bill had always treated Jesse like crap. He belittled him constantly and told him he could never do anything right. I imagine it messed up Jesse for a long time. I never tried to stop Bill."

"We talked about this before. You were young and most likely afraid of what Bill might have done to you if you tried to comfort Jesse." Brooke tried consoling her. "I'm going to keep saying it until you understand that it wasn't your fault."

"I know," Shelly replied. Not yet crying, but just on the edge of tears. "After Bill died, things seemed to settle down for a little while. Do you remember that trip we made here to Idaho and to California to visit you?"

"I sure do," Brooke replied. "Now, looking back on it, I can't believe you and the kids made the entire trip on your own."

Shelly talked of the things they did on that trip. She told her about seeing Yellowstone and Old Faithful. She then told Brooke about stopping at state lines to take pictures of the kids under the signs.

"I still have those photos. It seems silly now, but we had fun stopping at the state line signs. We jumped out of the car and I lined up the kids in front of the signs and took their pictures with a cheap camera."

She told Brooke how Jesse was fifteen and had his driver's permit. He was able to take turns with Shelly driving, but only in the less populated areas.

"We must've needed that trip to heal after Bill died, now that I look back on it. I won't get into that now. We can talk about that later because there are so many things I want to tell you before the whole story of how Bill died," Shelly said.

"That's a good idea," Brooke replied. "I know how sensitive that topic is."

Shelly composed herself again and began telling Brooke of another time with Jesse. The time when he moved out of the house while still in high school.

"He was around sixteen or seventeen and getting more independent. He didn't spend much time at home. One day, Jesse said he wanted to move in with his friends, the Kaufman brothers."

"I recall you telling me about them. Didn't you meet one of them the last time Jesse visited you?" Brooke recalled.

"Yes, that's right. They are a good bunch of guys. They all have grandkids and live not too far from my apartment. Maybe within an hour, give or take. When Jesse came up recently, we met one of the Kaufman brothers for lunch," Shelly said.

"Anyhow. I didn't really say much to him when he told me he was moving in with them back then. I figured they would be okay because Jesse and the Kaufman boys attended the same high school. Looking back on it, I should have never let him leave."

"Shelly, had you kept him there, do you realize that his life may have been different today? If I remember right, didn't he find his career and his passion, while he was living with them?" Brooke reasoned. "Besides, the seventies were far different from today."

"I guess you're right about that," Shelly said.

Satisfied with her reasoning, Shelly discussed another time about her and Jesse.

"Looking back at another time when Jesse brought Mary and little James, who was just a toddler, out to Idaho. Jason and I lived out there then. I think I drove him away by being too controlling. I didn't think at the time that I acted that way with them. Here, I thought I was doing what a mother should do. I tried to help him by making suggestions about his work, and suggestions to help him and Mary with little James." Shelly said.

"It goes back to co-dependency, doesn't it?" Brooke suggested.

"It sure does. I never had a clue I was doing this to the kids."

"Shelly, I never knew I was doing it to my kids, Mark or Adam," Brooke added.

After Brooke comforted Shelly, reminding her of the co-dependency issue with Jesse, Shelly continued. "Well! I wanted to see Jesse do well. Any mother wants the best for her kids. They had found a small mobile home to live in about two miles away from us in town. I started trying to find little side jobs for his business, but didn't realize that it was pushing him away. I was trying to help by making suggestions on what they could feed James since he was just a young boy even though they weren't asking for my help ."

"What you were doing and what I was doing were very similar," Brook added. "We never realized it then."

"Nope. It all came to a head one day when I tried calling their home and the phone line was disconnected. Jason drove over there and found the mobile home empty."

A relative of Shelly's called her and told her she had received a phone call from Jesse. He explained to them why they had to leave like they did. The relative told them that Jesse had moved to Florida.

"Jesse told her he felt trapped. He said I was trying to control him and had to get out. I didn't realize I did that to them. Here, I thought I was helping them. I was mad for a long time because he just up and left with his family and never said goodbye or that he even had to leave. After looking back on it, I guess I can understand. For what he did for his profession, he belonged in Florida, but I still have a little trouble dealing with how he left. I think I am beginning to understand how he felt and why he had to get away. Idaho just wasn't the right fit for him. It must have been what I was doing to him and that he wanted to get back to Florida that ended up being too much. He had to leave as fast as he could."

Brooke said, "It's natural to want to get out of something as fast as possible when someone feels trapped."

"I know, but it's still hard to accept that he was trying to get away from me when I thought I was helping."

Shelly still felt guilty and saddened while accepting that it had happened.

"But all that was in the past, and you both are good now and have been good for quite a long time," Brooke said.

"Yep. Thanks to what Gary did," Shelly added. "To be honest, it was Gary who was responsible for some of the good things that happened to us. I'll get into that later, most likely tomorrow. It's getting late, and I'm getting sleepy. Just to finish up about Jesse, he has come up to visit me several times now. When Jason and I lived near him and Mary in Florida, he always came over and visited and to see if there was anything he could do for us."

"The Lord works in his own way to make things work out, doesn't he?" Brook confessed. Shelly agreed.

Jesse and Shelly had never discussed the day he, his wife, and their little boy, James, left like they did many years ago. Shelly thought it was best to leave things alone, since their relationship now was much better. With that, Brooke and Shelly got ready for bed. It was enough to wear them down, even though they had spent most of the day talking, especially at their age.

Before going to their bedrooms, Shelly gave Brooke a big hug. "Goodnight, Brooke. You do not know how I needed this today."

"There's more tomorrow, but we've made good strides today. Goodnight, sis."

As she climbed into her bed, Shelly laid her head on the pillow and felt a little better. She felt more free, more weight off her shoulders. As she lay in bed, her thoughts floated around her mind of the different things she and Brooke talked about. Shelly thought she would stay awake through part of the night because of it, but exhaustion overcame her, and it was not long before she was sound asleep.

GARY

Shelly woke up and smelled the aroma of coffee in the air. The smell awakened her from a good night's sleep. After waking up, she walked out to the kitchen in her light yellow pajamas with floral print. Brooke stood there, leaning on the countertop, holding a cup of coffee stretched out to Shelly. She took the cup and thanked her.

"Good morning, sleepyhead. How did you sleep?" Brooke asked.

"Better than I've slept in quite a long time. Thank you for asking."

"Well, that's good to hear, because we have more to discuss today. It's going to be a long day, and you need energy. Remember that you're going to talk about Gary and what he did for you and Jason. Speaking of Gary, He didn't come over yesterday, so he will most likely drop by today."

"That'll be nice. I'd prefer to tell you what he has done before he gets here," Shelly said.

"I'll fix a quick breakfast, and we can get settled into our spots in the living room."

Brooke mixed up four eggs with chopped bell peppers, onions, and a handful of small chunks of ham into a scrambled egg dish. After cooking the meal, she delivered a small plate of eggs and a piece of buttered toast to Shelly. Brooke walked into the kitchen again, got her plate ready, and went into the living room to eat with Shelly.

After they finished breakfast, Brooke took the dishes to the sink in the kitchen, where she washed the plates and put them in the dishwasher to dry. Brooke often used the dishwasher, but occasionally, when she did not have many dishes, she just washed them by hand and stack them in the dishwasher for drying. Afterward, she returned to the sofa, where Jonah was waiting for her.

Shelly started the conversation after Brooke sat at the end of the sofa. "Sometime back in the early 2000s, I don't recall when. Gary called Jesse's wife and talked to her about Jesse and me not speaking to each other since our falling out in the 90s."

Mid-2000s. Shelly and Jesse have not talked to each other since the incident in Idaho. Not wanting this to continue, Gary is determined to get his big brother Jesse and his mom back on speaking terms. Even if it starts out as just copying each other on social media and sending things such as funny pictures back and forth.

Gary picks up the phone and calls Jesse in Florida. He considered for a few moments what he might say, whether it was Jesse or Mary who answered the phone.

The phone rings at Jesse's house. "Hello," came a woman's voice. Mary answered the phone.

"Hi Mary. Gary here."

"Hi Gary. Nice to hear from you. How is the family?"

"Doing well, thanks. The children are getting bigger," Gary replied. "How is everybody doing there?"

"Well, the kids are a pain sometimes, but they are good most of the time." Mary chuckled, as did Gary.

Gary got to the main reason he called.

"Well, the reason I'm calling is about Mom and Jesse. This rift between them has gone on long enough. We need to get them back on speaking terms."

"I agree. It's been way too long," Mary said. "Do you have any ideas about how we could do it?"

Gary thought about this earlier, before the phone call. For a couple of days, he's thought of ways to get them to start talking to each other again and came up with one good idea. "I was thinking that sometimes, Jesse can include mom in the social media postings the same way he does with me. Hopefully, that might start the ball rolling in getting them to talk. Well, maybe baby steps."

"Sounds like a good idea. I'll suggest that to him, and I don't think it should be much of a problem," Mary said.

"Great! Let's hope this works."

Shelly finished telling Brooke the short story. "It wasn't long after that call from Gary that I started receiving postings shared by Jesse. I think I cried when I got his first message. I was so happy. Things got better in a short time. At a later time, he brought Michelle up with him to stay with us in Indiana for a visit," Shelly said. Michelle is Jesse and Mary's youngest child out of two.

"That was the second time that Gary did something wonderful that changed our lives. Up at the campground area where we stayed the summers, northwest of Fort Wayne, we hosted a family reunion. Gary and Jessica came along with their kids; Liz and Kevin came, and Jesse brought Michelle up with him. Melanie and her family lived about forty minutes away, so they came up as well. Mary stayed back with James since he had baseball and couldn't join Jesse and Michelle," Shelly said. "Liz and Kevin's kids didn't come with them. Anthony and Kelly were busy with their own lives. I wanted them to come, but I understood." She still felt sad and disappointed.

Shelly understood, since they were living in different states across the country. She was happy all of her kids could make the trip.

"There was a day where Melanie and her family and Jason's two daughters, Connie and Tina, came over to the camp ground to join the rest of us. We had a big cookout, everyone enjoyed swimming at the pool, and we took family photos. We needed to do this, as I didn't think we could ever get the entire family together like that."

"I bet it was wonderful. It must have been so emotional and if I were there, I would have been in tears."

"I cried a little, but I did it when no one could see. I didn't want them to worry about me or put a damper on the party. Things were going so well," Shelly said.

She continued telling Brooke about that day. About Jason and Jesse fighting over the grill and who gets to do the cooking on it. Everyone laughed. Both of them love cooking on the grill, although Jesse is better at it. He would prepare and season the meat. Jason stood at the grill and turned whatever meat was on there while Shelly did the prep work.

"You know how Liz is always the life of the party and can get anyone talking. Well, imagine having three of them that are the same way. Jason's two daughters are like that. That evening, the beer was flowing, and those three had everyone in stitches from laughing so hard. I laughed so hard I must have come close to peeing my pants. Gary fell off his chair once, and that made everyone laugh even harder."

"Those are the times we always cherish, you know?" Brooke added. "God must have lent an enormous hand in getting everyone together."

"I think so. The next part where Gary came into play was on a different day at the campground. Jesse and Michelle were still there, as were Liz and Kevin. We were in the small living room talking. Jason mentioned the weather and that he was not looking forward to winter here again," Shelly said.

Jason and Shelly were getting older. The harsh winters in Indiana and Idaho had taken their toll on them. They lived in Fort Wayne during the blizzard of 1978. There were snow drifts so high next to the house they could touch the drift from the second-story bedroom windows. The house featured two front doors that opened inward with no screen door. When Jason opened the doors after the snow storm, there was a high wall of snow that took everyone of us a few days to dig out.

"Not long after Jason said he was sick of winter, Gary chimed in. Out of the blue, he asked why don't we move to Florida to where Jesse and Mary live. Jesse was there, and he got a big smile and said that would be great. Both Gary and Jesse went to the laptop on the desk and started searching for places to live near them. They didn't waste any time."

Shelly continued to tell Brooke about the move and how they found a cozy park model home in a retirement community about four miles from Jesse and Mary's house.

"When we moved there and for the entire time we lived there, Jesse would stop by our place at least a couple of times a month. He would check on us to see if we needed anything. It was so nice to have my oldest son back in my life," Shelly said, tearing up a bit.

Shelly and Jason lived in Florida near Jesse and Mary for seven years. Throughout that time, Shelly and Jesse's relationship had been solid. Shelly and Jason hosted several get-togethers over those years. Most of them also including Liz & Kevin, and Gary, Jessica, and their two kids.

In December, about five years ago, Jason received terrible news. He had been feeling tired and had low energy before the doctor's visit. Shelly took him to the doctor to see what the problem was. When the doctor saw something that concerned him, he ordered tests for Jason.

"I was terrified of what they were going to find. Jason's side of the family has a history of cancer. Dad had emphysema, and I saw what it did to him. I was afraid Jason might have cancer and afraid of what he might have to go through with the cancer."

A week later, the doctor called Shelly on the phone and that the results were in. The doctor asked for her and Jason to come into his office. The news was not good. Jason found out he had stage four Non-Hodgkins lymphoma. Jason sighed and asked what he could do and if there was a cure. The doctor said that chemo could prolong his life for about a year. Although, at this stage of the lymphoma, Jason would have about six months to live without the chemo. Give or take a month or two.

The news devastated Shelly. She was facing another tragic loss of a close family member. Her brother, her mom, her first husband, her dad, and now this. It terrified and saddened her. Jason, apparently, took the terrible news slightly better than Shelly.

"That is where Gary came in again and changed our

lives. Melanie and her family came down to see us in February. It was more like saying goodbye to Jason than a typical visit. They could only stay for a week because the kids, Lisa, and Nate, had to get back to school. Melanie cried several times in the bedroom, but not in front of her dad. She wanted to be strong for him. Then Gary flew to see us in March. He flew out alone because the kids were still in school, so Jessica had to stay back. Luckily, Kevin and Liz had also flown out around the same time."

"I bet that was comforting to Jason," Brooke added.

"It was. Especially one night when we were all doing Wii bowling. Kevin had a few beers in him, and you know how funny and crazy he can be," Shelly added.

"I can imagine what Kevin was like that night," Brooke replied.

"He put on this ridiculous pair of long-john underpants that were big and baggy. When he started clowning around as he does after drinking, he made Jason laugh so hard," Shelly said about that night.

Jason and Shelly knew he did not have long to live. What Kevin had provided for Jason that night showed that laughter really was the best medicine for the soul. It lifted his spirits, along with everyone else's. Everyone knew the laughter would not cure him, but for that evening, it improved the quality of Jason's life.

"I will never forget that night and what Kevin did for Jason and his emotional well being. Well, Liz and Kevin had to leave and fly back home to California. After they left, Gary continued to stay up several nights watching over Jason while he was in his hospital bed that hospice had for him in the living room. When Jason needed to use the bathroom or watch over him as he tried to sleep, Gary was there to help. I don't think he slept much while he was there."

"I'm not surprised that Gary did that for Jason and you," Brooke said.

Liz and Kevin had stayed long enough at Shelly and Jason's to see some of what Gary did to help Jason. "Liz told me later that she and Kevin were so impressed with the way Gary was helping to take care of him. The patience he had with Jason made her feel a swell of pride for what Gary had done for him. When Liz told me that, I felt proud of my baby boy."

"I would be proud of him, too. I think I can imagine all that he did to help Jason." Brooke commented.

"Well, Jason and Gary were sitting on his hospital bed in the living room and talking one day while Shelly was visiting with a neighbor out in our sunroom."

Early 2018. Gary had flown by himself to Shelly and Jason's in Florida. It was about the middle of March. Jessica and the kids had to stay back in Idaho. The kids had school and could not get away.

Gary's trip was to be more of a visit to say goodbye to his stepdad, Jason. They had been very close over the last forty-plus years. He and Jason had worked at the same place when Gary was in high school. Jason was one of the assistant managers at the restaurant where they worked. Several years later, Jason painted houses with his brother. Gary worked for him a little while until he got back on his feet. They would have fun teasing each other and playing some silly games. One of those was a game called buck seven that included farting and hitting the arm seven times after a fart if they said the word buck seven before the other said safety. Shelly never liked when we played game.

One sunny and warm day during March in Florida, at their park home, Gary and Jason sat on the side of Jason's hospital bed set up in their living room. The living room was the best option for the hospital bed. Shelly could monitor him, and it was easier to serve him his meals and for Jason to watch TV.

Shelly was visiting with a neighbor lady in their sun room connected to the back of the park home. Gary and Jason had begun a heart-to-heart talk. One they had never had the chance to have since Gary arrived.

"This whole thing stinks, Jason. It just isn't fair," Gary said. It saddened him that a great guy like his stepdad, Jason, was terminally-ill and did not have long to live. Gary wanted to scream but he didn't. He needed to be strong for Jason.

"I know," said Jason. "I just can't do anything about it." He sat on the edge of the bed, slumped over, and had a sort of defeated look to him. He knew the end was coming soon and felt helpless to do anything about it.

"Both you and Mom are living in limbo. You're just waiting to pass on, and Mom is waiting, not really knowing what to do in the meantime. It just isn't fair to either of you," Gary said.

Jason started shedding tears. His shoulders shook up and down and he let out a small cry that lasted a few seconds. Gary had never known him to cry. He had seen Jason cry one other time when his mom, who was in her nineties, passed away. Gary put his arm around Jason's shoulders. At that point, Jason broke down, crying even harder. They sat there for a few moments. Gary kept his arm around Jason's shoulders, comforting him while he wept. He came close to crying with Jason, but knew he needed to be strong for him.

Gary looked at Jason. "It's not fair to keep mom in limbo, and it's not fair that you just have to wait down here with no other family. All of your daughters are back in Indiana." He thought a little after he spoke to Jason.

Gary then sat up a little straighter and had a sudden thought: an epiphany. "I have an idea."

Jason was still looking down when he asked, "What is it?"

"Instead of staying down here and waiting for the inevitable, why don't you and mom move back to Indiana as soon as possible?" Gary said. "The sooner you both move there, the more time you can spend with the family and relatives up there."

Jason looked up at Gary, tears clearing up, shook his head up and down, and replied, "I like that. I can spend the remaining time I have with my girls and grandkids. Three months with them is better than nothing. I like it. Let's wait until your ma finishes visiting with the neighbor."

Jason's mood brightened instantly. His back straightened up. He wiped the remaining tears from his cheeks. Jason had a sense of purpose now. They just had to wait to tell Shelly about their idea and see what she thought.

As Jason and Gary sat on the edge of the bed chatting and talking more about it, Shelly was finishing up her visit with the neighbor lady. It was about ten minutes later, when the neighbor left through the sunroom door to the outside, and Shelly came in through the sliding door into the living room.

"Mom, we have something to ask you." Gary spoke out.

"What is it?" Shelly asked.

"Jason! Do you want to ask her, or do you want me to?"

"Naw. You go ahead," Jason replied as he waved his hand outward.

Shelly saw that Gary and Jason seemed to be in a better mood. She saw now that Jason's eyes seemed to sparkle and have some life in them. Shelly wanted to find out what had changed. She wondered what had happened while she was outside visiting.

Gary told Shelly what he and Jason had talked about earlier and the plan.

"Mom. With all that I told you, what do you think about you and Jason moving back to Indiana to spend the rest of his days? You wouldn't have to worry about trying to move back up there after he passes away, and you would already be situated in a nice apartment."

Jason added, "And I would get to spend the rest of my time with my girls and visit the grand babies."

Shelly smiled. "I'm in. Let's do this. I'm ready now." Her mood changed, and she didn't even have to think about it. Her excitement grew immensely. She loved spending time in Florida and spending quality time with Jesse, Mary, and their two kids. She had already planned on moving back to Indiana after Jason passed away.

Shelly was so ready to move that, after answering their question, she hurried into the kitchen and started packing what she could pack that they wouldn't need day to day. She didn't even think about it or what she needed to do. Shelly had moved so many times in the past to so many places throughout her life that she instinctively knew what to do. Shelly had Gary call the local businesses to get the utilities services canceled.

After working in the kitchen for a little while, Shelly realized she needed to call her youngest daughter, Melanie, to tell her the news. Jason called Connie and Tina to tell them about the big news.

Connie and Tina had their flights scheduled at different times to spend time with Jason and say goodbye before he passed away. Now things were different. They were now flying down to Florida to bring their dad home.

Gary had to fly back home to Idaho a few days after they decided to move back up to Indiana. He was able to do a lot in those two days. Gary had helped them pack up a bunch of things and get all the services scheduled for cancelation. Just before Shelly took him to the airport, both she and Jason told him how much they loved him and appreciated what he had done for them. Gary was glad to help in any way he could.

Tina came down first and helped with whatever needed to be done. She worked hard and did most of the packing for them. Tina told Shelly to let her do most of the heavy lifting and for Shelly to tell her what needed packing and which boxes they should go into. They had also sold and donated a lot of items that she and Jason had accumulated throughout their long marriage. By the time Tina left to fly back home, she had managed to get most everything packed up except for the basic things they needed.

Before Connie flew down from Indiana and while Tina was in Florida helping her pack, she and Melanie worked to find an apartment for Jason and Shelly, and they set up hospice care for Jason.

Shelly's oldest son, Jesse, came over to help with the packing whenever he could get away from work. Mary would also come with him sometimes to help with packing the smaller, more delicate items that needed wrapping. She also brought meals over to help, since most of the kitchen was being packed up. The food Mary brought over helped a lot. Shelly didn't have to worry about any of the cooking.

Jason's oldest daughter, Connie, flew down to Florida after her and Melanie found the apartment and got hospice care ready in Indiana. Things were all set. They already listed the park model home with a realtors' office and were ready to sell. Shelly and a friend were going to drive the moving van and the car up to Indiana. Connie flew back up to Indiana with Jason to get him settled into the new apartment. His failing health would not allow him to sit in a car for two days. The flight was only a few hours long, and it's a direct flight. The flight attendants put him in the front row. They made sure his small oxygen tank was secure.

What is remarkable is that from the time that Jason and Gary asked Shelly if she wanted to move back up to Indiana to the time they all arrived in Indiana had only taken two weeks. The park model home didn't sell for another couple of months, but they didn't mind.

"So you see, Brooke, Gary had pretty much been re-sponsible for us moving those different times when they all ended up being beneficial to us," Shelly said, beaming with pride.

"Shelly, it seems that God was working through Gary and I'm not sure he was aware of it," Brooke added. Shelly nodded in agreement.

Brooke and Shelly chatted for a little while longer about Gary.

Then the doorbell rang out.

THE SURPRISE VISITOR

Shelly and Brooke were lounging in the living room when the doorbell rang. Both ladies knew it was likely Gary at the door. He mentioned he might come over today.

"Stay right there, Shelly. I'll get it," Brooke said as she left to answer the door.

Shelly nodded to Brooke and grabbed her coffee mug for another refill. After she filled up her cup, she walked back to her chair. She looked over at the hallway to see if Brooke was coming back. Shelly noticed she had been at the door longer than expected and wondered if she should check on her, but waited a little longer.

After more time passed, she saw someone move through the entryway hall door and into the other smaller den- between the living room and the entry hall. The second living room, somewhat darker than the main living room. Shelly could tell it wasn't Gary, but a woman walking toward her, and she couldn't make out her face.

Must be the neighbor coming to visit, Shelly thought. As the woman got halfway through the other room, she saw Gary behind her. She still didn't see the woman's face and didn't respond.

As soon as the unrecognized lady walked into the main living room, where Shelly was sitting, the woman spoke.

"Well, hello, mom."

Shelly stared in shock and disbelief. Liz, her daughter, all the way up from California, was standing in front of her. She did not believe her daughter was standing before her.

"Oh, my goodness." Shelly smiled, laughed, and teared up at once at the wonderful surprise.

Liz leaned over to hug Shelly while she remained seated. Shelly still laughed and cried at the same time. She finally stood up out of her chair after the first shock and gave Liz an enormous hug.

"Never did I imagine you would fly up here. You told me you and Kevin were so busy. Busy with your kids and grandkids and what they had going on," Shelly said, sniffling and wiping her nose with a tissue.

"It surprised me when Gary motioned me outside, and Liz stood by the door," Brooke said.

While Shelly and Brooke sat in the living room, the doorbell rang. Brooke walked through the house to answer it. She opened the door, expecting Gary to be standing at the door. Brooke saw him, but he stood on the landing at the top of the three-step staircase, holding his finger to his mouth, telling Brooke to be quiet. She looked at him, puzzled. *What in the world is he doing?* she wondered.

Gary started motioning for Brooke to walk out through the door. He pointed for her to look at the bottom of the three steps that lead to the door.

Brooke followed his motion, looked at the bottom of the steps, and noticed Shelly's daughter and her niece Liz standing there. Brooke raised her hands to her mouth and began quietly crying. She grabbed Liz in a big hug, looked at Gary, and in a hushed tone, "You don't know how much this means to your mom and me." Gary nodded at her comment.

After the hug, Gary, Liz, and Brooke walked into the hallway by the main door of the big double-wide home. It was still out of view where Shelly was sitting. From there, they moved into the main part of the house, into the hallway that led into the small den before the living room. Liz walked ahead first, followed by Gary and then Brooke.

Shelly looked over at us coming through the den. Gary noticed his mom had not recognized Liz yet. The room they walked through didn't have any lights on in it. It shaded the three of them compared to the room where Shelly was sitting.

As Liz, Gary, and Brooke walked into the main living room, Liz said, "Well, hello, Mom."

Shelly recognized her at once after Liz spoke. Tears flowed while she laughed and cried at the same time. She was still somewhat surprised and stayed seated in her chair.

Liz walked over to Shelly, leaned over, and hugged her. Shelly then stood up after the first shock and tightly hugged her daughter while tears streamed along her cheeks. "Oh my goodness, " Shelly said.

After the laughing and crying settled a bit, Shelly asked, "Heaven's sakes, what a great surprise! Did you and Gary set this up?"

"We sure did," Liz answered.

Shelly expressed her happiness regarding Gary showing up with Liz. They stopped their embrace but still had an arm around each other, standing side by side. Shelly kept staring at Liz in disbelief, grinning from ear to ear.

Gary leaned over to Brooke. "I wondered that if you don't have room for Liz, she can stay at our place. I can just drive her back and forth to help you." Gary and Jessica lived close enough. The travel time would be only fifteen or twenty minutes each way. He's glad to drive Liz from his house to Brooke's.

"Oh no. Liz has to stay. We need her here. I'll fix up something where she can sleep."

"That sounds good," Gary said. He understood Brooke's

insistence on Liz staying there. She should be able to add lots of information from their past to help Shelly through her depression.

Brooke, Gary, and Liz sat in the living room with Shelly and began talking about the surprise visit. Gary and Liz told Shelly and Brooke how they put it together.

Shelly started first. "How did you both set this up?"

"Gary and I were talking on the phone about you coming out to visit and your depression. About how bad it was getting. We were worried about you. I said I'd try to make it up there, but Kevin and I were busy. Gary asked if there was any way I could even get two or three days to fly up to Idaho. I said maybe. So he got on the computer during the phone call and looked at several flights for me. I talked to Kevin about the trip, and we chose a flight that worked out the best. Kevin wanted to fly up, but he figured he'd just get in the way. Mom, he knew both you and I needed to get together."

"I really needed this. I didn't think you were going to make it up here because of your busy schedule," Shelly said.

"Do you remember Becky from Kelly's wedding?" Liz asked.

"Yes, I do," Shelly answered.

"She and I had plans. I told her I wanted to catch a flight here and asked if she'd be okay with canceling the plans. Becky was fine with it and encouraged me to get the ticket to fly up to see you," Liz told Shelly and Brooke.

Gary added, "I drove to pick her up at the airport and then we drove straight here. I kept it a secret from you and Aunt Brooke. Both of your reactions to seeing Liz here were priceless."

Both Brooke and Shelly expressed their complete surprise. They never could have dreamed of a more perfect outcome for the day.

"Liz, I have a question about when we texted each other last week. I texted that I wished you could be here, and you texted back that you were just too busy. Did you already have the ticket?" Brooke asked Liz.

"Yep, but I couldn't let on that I was coming up there." Liz and Gary determined it was going to be a complete surprise to Shelly and Brooke.

"Well, you little stinker," Brooke replied. Everyone laughed. After the laugh, Gary recognized this as a sign that it was time for him to leave.

"Well, I had better go. I'll leave you all to visit and catch up," Gary said.

Everyone stood up and hugged Gary.

"Thanks, little bro. This surprise worked out just as we expected," Liz said while hugging Gary and giving him a peck on the cheek.

Next was Brooke. Hugging Gary, she said, "Thank you for bringing Liz. I think it will help your mom heal."

Shelly grabbed Gary in a big hug and said, "You kids really surprised me. Thank you so much." Gary did not reply, but just smiled instead.

After the hugs, Gary said one last goodbye, petted Jonah, and left.

MOM

After Gary left, the women talked about Liz's plane trip and how it surprised them. Brooke realized they had not eaten lunch soon after the conversation began.

"Oh my, we haven't had lunch yet. Liz, you must be starving after your flight," Brooke said with a sudden realization.

"I'm not too hungry, but I'll eat something. A sandwich or something quick will be fine." Liz had eaten something at the airport in California. The flight she took from Sacramento to Spokane went by fast and she wasn't hungry, but accepted the sandwich out of consideration.

"Shelly, how about you?"

"That'll work for me, too," Shelly answered.

Brooke walked into the kitchen and made ham sandwiches. Gathering the items needed, she put the sandwiches together. After putting the ham and mayonnaise back in the fridge, Brooke discovered a bowl of leftover potato salad. She took the bowl out and added a small spoonful to each plate. Who doesn't love a good homemade potato salad?

The women ate their lunch at the dining table. "This tastes good, aunt Brooke. Thank you." Liz replied, enjoying the food.

"It sure does," Shelly agreed. "It's hitting the spot."

"Glad you like it," said Brooke while enjoying her own sandwich.

Throughout lunch, no one talked much except for comments about the weather and current events. The ladies were glad to be there together and enjoyed each other's company.

After the women finished lunch and cleaned up the dirty dishes, they walked back to the living room. Shelly sat down in her usual chair, and Liz sat in the small, dark brown rocker they brought in from the other room. Brooke sat in her place at the end of the sofa. Soon after, Jonah jumped up on the couch and snuggled up against her leg.

Glancing at Liz, Brooke said, "Liz, you were telling us about what you and Kevin have been up to since you retired."

Liz and her husband, Kevin Harrison, have been married for 43 years. They met in California, in Kevin's hometown, near Chico. Liz and Kevin had two kids, Anthony and Kelly, who are now adults. Each of their kids has their own families. Both Anthony and Kelly are doing well in their career. Shelly brags about them all the time. In fact, she brags of her grandkids every chance she gets.

Kevin supports Liz all the time, and he's had an excellent relationship with her for decades. To Liz's brothers, Jesse and Gary, he had always been like a real brother instead of a brother-in-law.

"Well, since Kevin's retirement and mine, of course, we've been doing a lot of traveling. Sometimes too much." That got a laugh. Kevin and Liz have traveled all over the West, seeing the sights and spending time with their family. "Most of the travel is to spend time with the kids and grandkids."

"I wonder what it would have been like if Shelly and I had found husbands who supported us as Kevin did for you. He treats you so well. Come to think of it, both Jesse and Gary treat their wives well."

"If you and Mom found different husbands in the beginning, you wouldn't have such a great niece. Mom wouldn't have had such a wonderful daughter. Am I right?" Liz joked, leaning towards Brooke and raising her eyebrows in jest.

Brooke and Shelly laughed and agreed with Liz.

Feeling proud of her kids, Shelly added, "We have brilliant kids, don't we?"

"Yep, we sure do," Brooke replied.

The topic switched up a bit. Brooke wanted to get back to helping Shelly. She pondered for a moment where her and Shelly's troubles might have started.

"Shelly, I've been thinking that some of our problems and emotional issues could have begun with mom. Not all our problems, but I believe she played a big part."

"Honestly, I've never thought about it, but you could be right," Shelly replied. "One thing I distinctly remember is that mom always kept the house clean and set our meals on the table at the same time every day. However, I never remembered her showing us any affection or love."

"I remember that as well," Brooke added. "It's like she was just our caretaker and not much more."

"In fact, there was this one time when she walked out and was going to leave us. This incident happened before you were born." Shelly told the story to Brooke and Liz.

Early winter of 1946. The weather was cold with a gentle wind. A thin layer of snow blanketed the ground, leaving the dried grass poking out from the layer. The day was dark because of the heavy cloud cover. The past few days have been dreary and overcast. In a small house in rural Montana, 6-year-old Shelly Gallagher and her 4-year-old brother, Stevie, were in the living room on the sofa. It sat against the wall just below the big window that looked into the front yard.

Shelly and Stevie's parents, Marilyn and Jake Gallagher, were arguing in the kitchen near the front of the house, across the living room.

While her parents were fighting, Shelly sat on the couch playing with her doll, trying not to listen. She continually combed the doll's hair, trying hard not to hear the yelling. No matter how hard she tried, she could not shut it out.

Sitting next to her, Stevie played with his little toy horse. He trotted the toy across his lap and part of the couch, making little horse sounds. Stevie appeared oblivious to the arguing going on in the kitchen.

"I've had it with you and this life. I can't take it anymore!" Marilyn yelled. Her face flushed with anger. She was shaking from the adrenaline rush of anger coursing through her.

"What are you saying?" Jake asked. He tried to stay calm, but his words did not quite come out that way.

"I'm leaving and going back to mom and dad's until I can figure out what to do. I just can't take it anymore," she yelled.

Marilyn started walking toward their bedroom to pack. As she did, Jake stepped in her way, faced her, and grabbed each of Marilyn's arms in a gentle manner to talk her out of it. "Let's talk about this some more. Let's try to work it out," Jake said in as even a tone as he could, despite the tension. He had calmed down a bit more. His tone was calmer than Marilyn's.

Marilyn twisted a bit, took a small step back, and said in a low but stern voice, "Jake, get out of my way."

He shook his head a bit in resignation and stepped aside. Marilyn rushed past him without giving Jake a second look and headed to the bedroom. He stood there with his head hanging down, feeling defeated and wondering what else he could do to keep her from leaving.

While sitting in the living room, Shelly tried blocking out the argument. She was old enough to understand what was happening and glad Stevie wasn't aware of the arguing going on. At this point, he was living in his own little world, playing with a toy horse. Neither Jake nor Marilyn realized the stress they caused Shelly. They were hurting her emotionally. She hated seeing them fight. Maybe they thought she remained unaware of what was going on, just like little Stevie was unaware. Or perhaps they never thought of how it affected the kids during their argument.

After a few minutes, Shelly heard her mom walking out of the bedroom and into the hallway by the living room. She was wearing a long and heavy coat and a thick headscarf. One thing that stood out to Shelly was the small suitcase her mom was carrying. She wondered why her mother carried it.

"Mommy, where are you going?" Shelly asked. She was disconcerted by what was happening and what her mom was doing.

Marilyn said nothing. She just looked at Shelly, then turned her gaze to Stevie on the couch for a few moments. She turned her head to the door, looked downward in contemplation, and started walking for the door.

Jake followed her. He looked over at Shelly and tried

to smile to reassure her. It did not work. Even at her young age, she could see his smile was fake.

"Stay here and watch Stevie, ok?" Jake directed Shelly.

"Ok!" Shelly replied. She turned, walked back into the living room, and joined Stevie on the couch. Shelly saw Stevie was oblivious to what had been happening between Jake and Marilyn. She sat down on the sofa next to Stevie and joined him as he played with the toy horse. She hoped it would keep him distracted. Perhaps it was more to keep her distracted.

Shelly heard the door open and shut while sitting on the sofa. She turned around on the sofa, kneeled, leaning against the back, and looked out the window. Stevie turned around and joined her at the window to look at what his big sister saw. Shelly pointed out the window, showing him what she was looking at. She put a finger to her mouth, prompting Stevie to be quiet. Then both turned to the window and looked outside at their mom and dad.

Marilyn had walked outside through the front door with Jake following, desperately pleading with her. He was afraid she would leave him. Jake didn't know how to raise the kids on his own. "What can I do to make things right? Tell me," Jake pleaded.

Marilyn never stopped. She never answered him. She kept walking away from the house down the lane with her suitcase in hand. It would be a long walk in the chilly air in the early winter. The house they lived in was about three miles from town.

Shelly and Stevie saw their mom walking away from them. She never looked back at the kids. She never even looked back at the house. The lane to the road measured about a quarter of a mile long. Neither of the children said anything to each other. They just watched their mom walk away while carrying her small suitcase.

The kids saw that their mother stopped walking halfway down the driveway, on the cold and overcast day. When Shelly saw her mom stop, she straightened up. She became hopeful that her mom would come back to the house.

Marilyn had stopped walking and hung her head down. She brought her free hand up to her mouth and wept. Her shoulders had slumped forward and shook. Marilyn wanted to keep walking away from the house and away from the marriage. She just couldn't take another step forward.

After a few moments, Marilyn turned around and walked back to the house. She still hung her head low and walked much slower than when she had walked away from their home minutes earlier. Her walking became more of a slow meandering along the lane toward the house.

Shelly saw her mom coming back and stood up a little higher on her knees. She was happy to see her mom coming back to the house. Shelly quickly got off the sofa, pulled Stevie with her, and walked over to the edge of the living room near the front door. She waited with Stevie for her mom to come back inside. Excited to see her mom walking back, little Shelly stood patiently waiting at the edge of the living room. She expected a big hug when her mom walks through the door.

Another couple of minutes passed by. Shelly's mother walked through the front door, followed by her father.

She knew the hug was coming soon. Shelly grew more excited with each passing second. Marilyn walked toward the living room. She didn't stop walking. Instead, Shelly's mother slowed down and glanced at Shelly and Stevie, giving them a slight smile. Marilyn then looked back down the hall and continued walking to the bedroom. Jake walked behind her and stopped in the living room. Shelly's mom walked inside the bedroom to put her suitcase away. Jake stayed with the kids and patted Shelly on the head, trying to be as comforting as possible.

Marilyn put away her clothes and suitcase, got out of her coat and scarf, and walked back out into the hallway. She walked toward the living room.

Mom is coming back out now. I'm going to get a big hug from her, Shelly thought. Marilyn went into the kitchen instead of going to the living room. Without saying a word to anyone, she put on her apron and started working. She never said a word to Shelly or Stevie about why she wanted to leave. Marilyn Gallagher gave no apology or reassurance that it wouldn't happen again.

"Good thing she came back, Aunt Brooke, or you wouldn't have been born," Liz said with a smile.

All three got a good laugh out of that comment. Liz meant it to be both funny and comforting.

"Shelly, was that the only time you recall?" Brooke asked.

"I think so," Shelly said. "But then again, I was quite older than you and left the house at around 16 when I married Bill. Also, there are a lot of things that slipped my mind from a long time ago."

Shelly and Brooke's mom, Marilyn, had left the family often. Each time she left, she would say she was not coming back. Something had changed her mind, and she would return. No one ever knew what had changed her mind each of those times. Was it leaving the kids behind for Jake to raise alone? What would they have to go through without her? Was it Jake, and whether she truly loved him? Had it been the thought that she would have to face the unknown of what might await her without her family? Marilyn never told anyone why she had always come back. She never even told her parents or siblings.

"Well, mom walked out on us several times. She always came back and acted as if nothing had happened, going about her cleaning or cooking. I never found out why she always left." Brooke said.

Shelly added, "Mom was always cooking and cleaning. Her food tasted good, especially her cinnamon rolls, and the house was always clean."

"We moved around a fair amount, and I never felt like we had a stable home. It was tough when mom killed herself." Brooke recalled. "That day, mom took me to the bus stop to make sure I got to school okay. About midway through school, aunt Gwen came and got me out of class. She told me that mom was in the hospital. I didn't know what really happened until later when someone else told me mom died. No one told me how she died. I eventually found out that mom sat down on the lower steps inside the house, took a shotgun, and shot herself in the chest. One of the older relatives found her laying on the stairs with a pool of blood around her, dripping down the steps. It hit dad hard, too. Things just got worse after that."

"Why didn't I help you when Mom died? You were only ten at the time." Shelly asked. "I should have been there for you."

"Oh, Shelly, I don't blame you at all. You had just gotten married to Bill and had your own family to work on."

"You are my family, Brooke. I should have done something," Shelly emphasized as she began tearing up.

Brooke stood up, walked to Shelly, and hugged her while she remained in the recliner, reassuring her she did not blame Shelly at all. In the past, and now, Brooke had never blamed her sister for not helping her or being there for her when she was young. She knew Shelly had her own life since she was a fair amount older than her. Brooke standing up to hug Shelly, helped comfort herself as much as it did for Shelly.

Liz sat close enough to Shelly that she reached over

and put a comforting hand on her mom's arm. Shelly looked back at Liz and let her know she appreciated her just being there and that she was doing a little better now.

Brooke walked back to the sofa after she'd had an emotional embrace with Shelly and sat back down next to Jonah.

"Shelly, I know you had your problems with Bill. I also had problems, and it was tough for me. We each had our own problems to deal with back then. I don't blame you one bit. I never did."

Dinner was closing in, and Brooke suggested they eat soon and continue the talk after the meal. Shelly and Liz all agreed.

CHAPTER 9

BROOKE- THE EARLY YEARS

After eating a wonderful dinner of spaghetti, garlic bread, and a small salad, Liz helped pick up the dishes from the table.

"Mom. You go in and sit down while I'll help aunt Brooke clean up."

"Are you sure?" Shelly asked.

"Yep! We've got this. Go."

After finishing the dishes, Liz and Brooke walked back out to the living room, where Shelly was sitting with a cup of coffee.

Liz sat in the glider chair, and Brooke took a seat at the end of the sofa. Like clockwork, Jonah jumped up beside her and laid next to her leg. Liz and Shelly comment how good the dinner was, and that they were both full.

"Aunt Brooke, before dinner, you were telling about the times you moved," Liz began.

Brooke started, "Well, you know the story of mom and how she died, right?"

"Before you told me the details, I'd only heard some stories of that, and of mom's stories of things that happened with her and dad before I was born. I never heard about what happened to you after your mom died," Liz said. Curiosity was growing stronger.

"Well, your mom had just recently gotten married, and our mom had taken her own life just two days before my tenth birthday. Shortly after her death, dad moved us to Sandpoint. The place we moved into was tiny. There were just two rooms. Not two bedrooms, but two rooms. There wasn't even a bathroom there, so we had to use the shared one at the end of the main hallway in the apartment building."

"That sucks," Liz said, feeling bad for Brooke.

"Dad was gone a lot for work. I was ten years old and had to cook for myself and get to school on my own. Because dad was always gone, I almost always came back to an empty apartment. I didn't have any friends at school since I was new, and there weren't any kids to play with around the apartments."

Shelly started tearing up and asked, "Why didn't I have you come live with Bill and me?"

"Shelly, you were just married, and besides, I got to

spend a few days with you once in a while. One time I spent about four or five days at your place once while you two lived in Spokane."

"I don't remember that. Geez, I am so forgetful. I can't even seem to recall important things from back then." Shelly murmured, wiping the tears from her eyes.

"Mom, it's okay. Everyone is different. You have trouble recalling things from the past, while I can recall things from a long time ago, like they were yesterday. But I have trouble remembering what I had for lunch yesterday," Liz said with a smile.

The small remark from Liz had broken the tension and made Shelly and Brooke laugh. She has always had that gift. Liz always seemed to realize when a cute comment would break the tension during emotional or stressful moments. If Liz was in the room, you'd bet that things would not be boring at all. She could make anyone feel at ease and comfortable.

"Shelly, I don't blame you. I was glad for those times that I could stay with you and Bill. I got to stay with my big sister. Believe me, it broke up the boredom and loneliness at home. Also, I was too young to think anything of it or to complain about it," Brooke said, trying to reassure her sister.

"Well, I never thought of it that way. But it's strange that I don't remember you being there and visiting. I had Bill to deal with, and how he treated me. How could I have put in that situation? It was either stay alone at home while dad was away all the time or stay here around Bill." Shelly said this while still shedding some tears.

"Bill was actually nice to me. He had a song he would sing to me, which always made me happy. I still remember most of the words, but I don't quite recall the catchy tune. At least it was catchy to me." Brooke mentioned this to Shelly and Liz.

Lincoln, Lincoln, I've been thinkin'
The very best place to go
is down to the store
to get a malt so our
bellies will be full.

"Wow, I'm jealous," Liz said, joking. "Sounds like Dad liked you more than he liked us kids. He never sang anything to us."

All the ladies laughed. Liz had made one of her usual jokes, but deep down she still thinks about her dad and wonders how he could've acted that way toward his own kids.

"Now, Liz. I'm sure your dad loved you. He just had his own way of showing it," Brooke said.

"Well, he had a funny way of showing it," Said Liz, still chuckling.

Brooke continued with her story. "After close to a year in Sandpoint, dad landed a job at the cattle auction yards in Walla Walla, Washington. For me, it wasn't hard to leave Sandpoint. That little apartment was depressing. I never made any friends there, and I always had to come home to fix my own meals and clean the apartment.

Dad didn't do much when he was there except drink that cheap wine and smoke those nasty cigarettes he rolled. But I suppose we have to keep in mind that mom had just died, and it was really hard on him. And I don't imagine he ever got over losing Stevie at such a young age. I imagine he was also tired from working a lot. Dad seemed to get hired at the more demanding jobs that wore him out.

"Brooke, I never knew you and Dad lived in Walla Walla," Shelly said. Surprised at the discovery, Shelly wondered what else she'd not been aware of about her sister.

"Neither did I," Liz said.

Learning about Walla Walla, Shelly felt even more ashamed that she knew little of what happened with Brooke in the early years. She told Brooke she felt horrible for not knowing about it and for not being able to help her.

"Shelly, it wasn't any of your fault, and I wish you would stop feeling guilty." Brooke said, comforting Shelly.

"Tell us about Walla Walla," Liz stated.

"Let me see... Dad and I moved there when I was eleven. The small place dad picked out had no furniture except for two beds. We didn't have any furniture in the living room. Dad never bought any because he was always busy at the auction yard."

Brooke continued to tell Shelly and Liz about the small place and the rooms. She told them it was an upgrade from the tiny apartment in Sandpoint since there were more rooms and even had its own bathroom. That was a big bonus for an eleven-year-old girl.

Brooke continued, "I wanted to be a cheerleader so bad. Since there was nothing in the living room to get in the way, I would practice and make up cheers and routines. At the time, I thought they were good. You both know how young girls think that everything they do is great."

Liz interrupted, "Not me. Everything I did was great." She winked at Brooke with a wry smile.

Shelly and Brooke broke out in laughter. Brooke replied with a teasing smile, "Of course you were. You were little Miss Perfect."

Shelly was shaking her head no, but with a little smile. Liz saw her and started laughing. "Gee, thanks, Mom."

Brooked continued, "But looking back, I'm glad we didn't have anything to record the cheer routines on. The routines were most likely pretty bad." She tried to think back to the routines she did, but she could not picture them in her head.

"The cheers might not have been as bad as you think, aunt Brooke. I bet they were pretty cute," Liz added.

"Thanks, Liz," Brooke replied. "Anyway, we had gotten a dog named Taffy. Taffy was a mutt, but I think she had a lot of Golden Retriever in her. When I wasn't practicing my cheerleading, I would go around trying to find scrap pieces of wood. I wanted to build her a doghouse. Once I realized I collected enough scrap wood, I got the hammer and nails that Dad had lying around and started working on it."

"How did it turn out?" Liz asked.

"I don't think I did a very good job on it and didn't know what I was doing. I missed the nail several times, and a few of those hit my finger instead of the nail. Good thing I didn't swing the hammer very hard," Brooke said as she raised her hand and moved her thumb back and forth.

Shelly and Liz laughed. Liz at once thought of her husband, Kevin, and how many minor mishaps he had while working on small building projects at their house.

"It seemed to work well enough because Taffy ended up sleeping in there. I'm surprised it didn't fall on her, but it held up well enough."

Brooke said she was thirsty and asked Liz and Shelly if they wanted something to drink. Liz had her water bottle, but Shelly said she could use another refill of coffee.

After Brooke returned with their decaf, she continued. "Ok. Continuing where I left off, that dog house held up for the rest of the time we lived there. No relatives were living nearby, like in Idaho, and since I didn't have anyone there besides Dad—and he was always working—I started collecting old pop bottles. I would grab my little red wagon about twice a week and start walking around neighborhoods and public trash cans, trying to find empty pop bottles. When I thought I had collected enough bottles, I would take them to the local grocery store for money."

"Jesse, Gary, and I did that as kids as well," Liz reminisced. "We had fun doing it. It was like a little adventure. We didn't have a wagon, though. We just put them in a box or a bag and carried them. At least Jesse and Gary carried them while I supervised." Liz finished with a little wink and a nod, which brought more laughter from Brooke and Shelly.

"Now imagine having to do it all by yourself in a town with no friends and nobody that you knew," Brooke stated.

"I couldn't even imagine." Shelly replied. She has never been in that situation of having no one else around like Brooke had experienced. However, she had gone through her own ordeals that Brooke was fortunate enough to have never experienced. Shelly would not wish those on anyone.

"At one point, dad taught me how to drive a big farm truck so I could help feed the cows. I was only eleven, and here I was driving the truck like an adult. The men at the cattle auction yard loaded up the truck with feed for the cattle. Then I would drive it out for the cows in the fields, get in the back, and shovel it out to them with a scoop shovel. It was fun watching all those cows come up behind the truck and eat the feed. It gave me something to do so I wouldn't have to stay home by myself all the time."

"Dad had married someone while you were in Walla

Walla, right? I think her name was Lois," Shelly said. "I don't remember you guys being in Walla Walla, but I knew he had married someone."

"That's right. Around six months after we moved there, Dad married Lois. She waited tables at a small diner close to the cattle yards. Two things that come to mind about her were how much she looked like mom. It was uncanny. The other was that she was very nice to me. Lois had saved up her tips and bought me a bicycle. I'll never forget that."

"What ended up happening to her?" Liz asked.

"I'm not sure what happened between her and dad. I can only guess that his drinking and the fact he hadn't gotten over mom's death may have driven her away," Brooke said.

"Didn't you go back up to Idaho after that?" Shelly asked.

"Yes, but not with Dad. He sent me back up there to live with aunt Irene and uncle Lee. I felt abandoned again. One consolation was that I got to be with my school friends again. Three girls became my best friends there. And I had a fair amount of decent friends as well. I got to stay there for two years, from around seventh grade to part of the way through ninth."

While Brooke was talking about her time with aunt Irene and uncle Lee, she could not help smiling while she did so. Brooke had some of the best times there during her entire childhood.

"I finally had a family with aunt Irene and uncle Lee

and the cousins. I still missed dad, but I wasn't alone at the house. But then dad came up to bring me back. It broke my heart."

Brooke was in her freshman year in high school up in north Idaho. She had been living with Irene, Lee, and her cousins for two years. For the first time in her life, she felt like she was in a loving home with a family. Her aunt and uncle treated her like one of the family members, like one of their kids.

She had her old friends at school from when she attended that same school as a kid. Brooke had her three best friends among them and was on the cheerleading squad. It was a lifelong dream of hers.

During Brooke's freshman year in high school, she got a letter from her dad. The letter said that he had remarried and that his new wife had her own kids. Jake wanted Brooke to come back home and live with them.

Tears slowly started trickling down her cheek from the corners of her eyes. The thought of having to move again weighed heavily on her. Brooke liked it there with her aunt and uncle and the cousins. Brooke had good friends and a good social life. She wasn't alone this time.

Brooke took the letter and showed it to her aunt Irene, Jake's sister. Irene saw Jake was driving up in about two weeks. "Aunt Irene, I don't want to leave. Please tell dad to let me stay here. Please!" Brooke pleaded.

Irene grabbed Brooke in a hug as Brooke began to cry. "Kiddo, we don't want you to go, but he's your dad. I have to go with what he wants."

"Maybe he'll forget or change his mind," Brooke hoped.

"Just wait and we'll see," Irene replied. "But for now, you just act as if you aren't going anywhere. Go to school. Spend time with your friends. We don't need to pack for you now. Instead, we can do that if the time comes."

Brooke stopped crying. "Thanks, aunt Irene. I love you," she said, wiping the tears away.

"Love ya' too, sweetie."

For the next few weeks, Brooke continued on with her life as if she were not leaving soon. She remained happy and content except for a gnawing deep in the gut that she may have to move again.

On a Saturday late in the morning, while Brooke was sitting out in the yard with her cousins, she saw an old truck come up the driveway. Brooke never saw the truck before, but something in her gut told her it was her dad coming to take her back to his home in California.

As the truck drove closer, she could tell it was her dad. Brooke developed mixed feelings upon seeing her father. She didn't know what or how to think. Brooke loves her dad but does not want to go with him. For the first time in quite a while, she was in a stable home with aunt Irene and uncle Lee. She had a great social life at school. How could she give that up?

When the truck stopped, Jake got out, smiled at Brooke, and in his calm, friendly, and casual way, he said, "Hello, Brooke." with a hand-rolled cigarette between his fingers.

Brooke walked over and hugged her dad. "Hi, dad. Missed ya'." Part of her was glad to see her dad, but the other part of her saddened at the realization of leaving. Jake could see this in her reaction. Brooke was glad to see him, but he could also see she showed some hesitation and mixed feelings.

"I missed you too. All ready to go?" Jake asked. He still looked the same as he had before she moved to her aunt and uncle's house. Brooke noticed her father had not put on any weight. He was still very thin. He still wore his old-style button-up cowboy shirt and blue jeans. Jake was also wearing his well-used cowboy boots. Brooke could never recall a time when he did not wear cowboy boots.

Brooke lowered her head and asked despondently, "Do I have to? Dad! I like it here and I have friends here; plus I'm a cheerleader. Please don't make me go."

"I'm sorry, Brooke, but I want you back home. Things'll be better this time, and you'll have more family than just me," Jake said. His new wife has kids of her own living with them.

"When are we supposed to leave?" Brooke asked.

"Well, I'd like to leave tomorrow morning. I have to get back to work as soon as I can," Jake answered.

"That doesn't give me any time to say goodbye to my friends! Please let me stay."

"Sorry, Brook, but I want you back home with me," Jake said, his voice sounding more convincing that this is better for her.

Brooke turned away and stormed off to the house. Turning back toward Jake, she proclaimed loudly and sternly, "This is my home," pointing her finger to the ground. Afterward, she stormed back inside the house and slammed the door.

Later that evening, Irene packed her two small suitcases with most of her clothes and toiletries. Irene found a small box to put the rest of Brooke's things in.

The morning came. Irene fixed breakfast for everyone. She wanted Brooke and Jake to have a good meal for their trip, so she fixed pancakes and sausage. Irene realized they had a long drive and would need food to help them during the drive. She packed them sandwiches, some snacks, and a thermos of coffee for Jake. Irene did not want Brooke to leave. She'd become part of the immediate family.

Brooke ate a few bites of the breakfast before her. Everyone could tell she didn't have an appetite. Jake ate a decent amount of food and thanked his sister. He was eager to get back on the road and head home.

It was finally time to leave. Jake and Brooke had a long drive ahead of them. Brooke's uncle Lee took out the suitcases and box and put them in the back of the old truck.

The whole family gathered outside to see Brooke and Jake off and say their goodbyes. Her cousins gave her big hugs. Tears were flowing.

Aunt Irene grabbed her in her arms and held her for a while. She looked at her niece with tears in her eyes and her voice choking up. "You take care of yourself now. Write to me when you can." After a sniffle, Irene continued, "I'm gonna miss you." Irene grabbed her again in a quick hug. Brooke could say nothing through her tears.

After Irene let go, Brooke turned to walk over to hug her uncle Lee. He was so nice to Brooke and treated her like one of his own kids. Something in her made her rush to him, and she wrapped her arms around her uncle.

Brooke started crying out loud. She clutched onto uncle Lee.

"I don't want to go," Brooke cried aloud. "Uncle Lee!" she cried more. "Don't make me go," clinging to him with all her might.

Lee was crying as he held his niece. "I want you to stay, too," Lee said, sobbing. "But your dad wants you with him. It has to be this way. Sorry, sweetheart. I wish you could stay with us."

Lee was a rugged man. He never cried. This morning was a rare occasion. Lee was the town cop and had worked up in the mountains doing logging in the past.

Brooke finally pulled away from him, realizing she was going to move again. She stepped back, and the crying ebbed to a slow trickle. She looked at everyone with sad eyes. Brooke knew there was no getting out of it.

Jake was waiting for her as she started walking to the truck. He had the passenger door open for her. Brooke got in, and as she sat down, her head lowered, and she began crying again, this time with more of a whimper. Her shoulders lightly shaking.

Jake said his goodbyes, got in the truck, and started driving down the lane.

Brooke wanted to look back one last time. She knew she would see them again in the future. They are her relatives. She couldn't bring herself to look at them at this moment. It would have been too much for her to handle.

"Wow! Aunt Brooke, I never knew... I'm so sorry you had to go through that," Liz said. There was a lot she never knew about Brooke's childhood.

"It led to me eventually meeting Adam. But that didn't happen until later. I didn't get along with my new stepmom, but I got along fine with her own kids. She wasn't only mean to me; she was mean to her kids as well.

In the middle of my Junior year, dad saw how bad it was for me, and he sent me back up to Idaho again. But this time I lived with aunt Gwen and uncle Gene. It was there I met Adam."

"You bounced around all over the place," Liz commented.

"I sure did. One day when I was with aunt Gwen and aunt Irene, one of them said that I had better be careful. They said my desire to have a family could get me pregnant before I finished high school. I was determined not to let that happen."

"I can see where they would be concerned," Shelly remarked. "After mom died, you never really had a stable home. You had to spend a lot of time alone."

Brooke nodded in agreement and then continued

with her story. "When Adam came along and we started seeing each other, I think I convinced myself that I would have no other chance to meet anyone else and get married. I thought that no one else would want me. I liked him well enough, but what I liked more was how nice his parents were. They treated me so well, and I saw they were nice to everybody."

Shelly was the first to notice how dark it was. She looked at the clock. "Oh my. Look at the time. It's getting late."

Liz looked at the clock on the wall as well. It said about 11 p.m.

"It's way past my bedtime," Shelly said.

Brooke nodded in agreement. "Let's continue this tomorrow. Not too early, though." They all laughed. "We need our beauty sleep."

All three ladies went to change into their sleepwear and brush their teeth. Afterward, they said goodnight and gave each other hugs. They each went to their rooms for the night.

BROOKE AND ADAM

The next morning, they woke up around the same time. Brooke walked into the kitchen to start the coffee. She noticed Liz had already beaten her there. "Well, good morning, Liz."

"Good morning, Aunt Brooke. Did you sleep well?"

"I sure did. How about you?"

"Not too bad," replied Liz. "I was trying to make the coffee but couldn't quite find it."

"See the little ceramic container? It's not marked, but it's in there," Brooke said.

As they started making the coffee, they heard Shelly come out of the bathroom. Both Brooke and Liz said good morning to her, and she replied.

"Want some coffee?" Brooke asked.

"Yes. It sounds good," Shelly replied.

A few minutes later, Brooke poured the coffee and handed a cup to each woman.

As Shelly got her cup of freshly brewed coffee, she leaned over the center island in the kitchen. "I slept like a baby last night."

"Oh, so you tossed and turned and pooped your diaper?" Liz replied jokingly and they all laughed.

Still laughing, Shelly said, "You know what I mean."

"Just having a little fun," Liz replied.

Brooke interrupted. "Who wants some breakfast? I have these little croissant breakfast sandwiches I can heat and serve."

Both Liz and Shelly said they would like one. After heating the sandwiches, they took the breakfast and coffee into the living room and sat in their chairs.

"Where did we leave off from last night?" Brooke wondered.

"You finished telling us about your childhood, and you wanted to tell us about the years with Adam," Liz said.

"That's right. When we first married, Adam didn't work much. I thought that was a little strange. All the men I knew, mostly my relatives, had always worked hard. Adam's dad had gotten him a job at a small local cannery in northern California. We lived there for about seven years. There were a lot of ups and downs. The boys were the ups, and Adam was mostly the downs."

Liz and Shelly laughed.

Brooke continued, "I became aware that some women from the cannery were having affairs with Adam, and I should have left him, but what could I have done? Where could I have gone with three young boys? Well, one day I found a bag of marijuana in his dresser drawer. I figured he must have been dealing and didn't see any other way that he was getting the money he had. I knew the cannery didn't pay that well."

Liz remarked, "That doesn't surprise me about him." Shelly stayed silent and just listened to her sister.

Brooke continued her story. "This is when I got close to God. I started taking the kids to church with me to get the strength to deal with Adam. I trusted God would save our marriage. I trusted that God would help keep our family together."

"Brooke, I didn't know any of this was going on," Shelly said. "I should have helped." Shelly was still feeling guilty for not being there to help Brooke when they were young. They had led different lives and had brief contact when they were younger, and Shelly was married at the time.

"Don't worry about it. At the time, I wasn't thinking right and was so narrowly focused. Anyway, we eventually separated, and I stayed in the little house, and Adam went to live with his parents. Then one day I heard a big rumble out front and saw a motorhome coming to a stop out by the yard."

Late in the year in 1979, on a Friday afternoon, Brooke's three boys, all in elementary school, were already out of school for the weekend. Brooke was sitting in the living room when she noticed a large RV pull up in front of their house next to the curb.

"Who could that be?" she wondered out loud, to no one in particular.

Brooke saw the motorhome door open as Adam stepped out of the RV. Brooke wondered what he wanted.

Could he be here to get me back? Is he here to start trouble? Is he going to take the boys away from me? Thoughts raced through her head.

Adam knocked on the door, and Brooke was right there to answer. The boys had come to the edge of the living room to see who it was. The kids were glad it was their dad. Adam said a quick hello to them with a wave and a smile. Then he looked at Brooke.

"Can I talk to you in the motorhome?"

"Sure," Brooke replied, having mixed feelings about this. She did not know what to think, but she was hopeful they would resolve their problems.

When they got into the motorhome, Adam turned to her. "I want to get back together because I have a plan for us. What I want you to do is this: pack a bag for you and the boys and go back up to Idaho. I'll send you up there on a bus."

Brooke was so overjoyed that she started crying and dropped to her knees. Her prayers had been answered. Brooke wrapped her arms around one of Adam's legs and buried her face in the side of his thigh.

"Thank you. Thank you. Oh, thank you," Brooke said through the crying.

What Adam did next caught Brooke off guard. He shook his leg that Brooke clung on to get her away from it and said coldly, "Oh, stop it already, woman." Then he turned away and walked into the house.

Brooke leaned forward, put her hands down on the floor of the motorhome, and began crying uncontrollably. What Adam did and said to her just now, hurt her deeply. Brooke was experiencing mixed feelings of getting back together with Adam and then the way he shook her off. She cried out to her long-since dead mother.

"Mom, I need you. Why did you leave me?" Tears streamed down her face. "Why didn't you love me enough to stay alive for me? Why?" crying out loud. Brooke felt betrayed and abandoned by her mom, who had taken her life several years ago. She never understood how a mother would do that and leave her own family that way.

Brooke continued crying for another few minutes. Once she calmed down, she wiped the tears from her face and left the RV to go into the house.

Adam was in the living room with the boys, talking to them. He was telling them about moving to Idaho.

With a voice firm and cold, he spoke to Brooke. "Go pack the suitcase for you and the boys now, and I am taking you to the bus station tonight. I'll stay back and sell the house and move up there when I'm done."

The sudden decision by Adam shocked Brooke. She

knew she couldn't trust him completely. But she trusts God. So Brooke began packing what she thought she and the boys needed for the bus ride. Two suitcases and her purse were all she had packed. Traveling with more than that would be difficult to handle. It brought back memories of when her father drove up to Idaho when she was a freshman in high school and took her back with him to California.

She didn't have time to phone her friends in the area or officially remove her children from school because it happened so quick. She was going up to Idaho in the early winter. It was cold up there compared to California. She realized the boys left their heavier jackets at the school. So she dressed them as warmly as possible, using multiple layers.

"Are you ready to go?" Adam asked.

Brooke looked at him with eyes heavy with sadness. "Yes."

"Get in the motorhome, and I'll take you to the bus station."

Brooke and the boys got in the RV. The boys remained silent. They may have been able to perceive what was going on between their mom and dad. Brooke got in and sat down in the back with the three boys. She did not join Adam up front in the passenger seat.

Arriving at the station, they all walked inside, and Adam went to the counter to buy their tickets. When he finished, he walked to the waiting area and spoke to Brooke.

"The only bus leaving tonight doesn't go into Idaho, but goes to Spokane instead. It leaves in about an hour. You can call Aunt Gwen or Aunt Irene when you get there or someplace on the way."

"What about money for food on the trip?" Brooke asked. "We'll need to eat something on the way."

Adam looked bothered by this, but he reached into his wallet and gave her some money. It wasn't much. The small amount disappointed Brooke, but she didn't want to complain. She would make do. "*God will help me,*" she thought.

"I have to get things ready for the move," Adam said as he leaned over and lightly grabbed Brook by the shoulders and kissed her on the cheek. "Bye Brooke. See you soon." Then he pulled away rather abruptly and moved over to the boys. He hugged them and said his goodbyes.

"Listen to your mom. Ok?" Adam said to his sons.

"Ok," they all said at the same time.

Adam turned and walked out the door. Brooke didn't believe he was leaving them alone to wait for the bus. She called out to him.

"Adam! Wait! Can't you stay with us until the bus leaves?"

"I can't. I've got work to do. You'll be fine here. Bye." Adam said this and then turned to leave. No more emotion had come from him than if he were going to the local store for a few minutes.

Brooke stood there, stunned. Many thoughts raced through her head. *Was he going to meet us up there? Was he sending us away for good?* She decided to put her faith and trust in God. Even though she was not sure about trusting Adam, she trusts God, and she trusts the trip up to Idaho will be the right one.

After some time had passed inside the bus station, there was an announcement for people to board the bus to Spokane, Washington. Brooke did not want the two older boys to be separated from her and Cecil on the bus. Even though the boys were all in elementary school, there was enough of an age gap between the two older sons and the youngest that she needed to watch out more for Cecil.

She gathered the suitcases and told the boys to follow her. Brooke gave the tickets to the driver and handed the suitcases to the attendant for storage. She then told the oldest boy, Larry, to find two empty rows of seats on the same side. As they walked down the bus aisle, Larry pointed to two rows on the left side.

"Mom, I found some seats," Larry said.

"Good! You and Brian take the two seats in the front, and Cecil and I will take these two behind you."

"Ok, Mom," replied Larry.

After the bus finished loading people and their luggage, they were on their way. Brooke had fixed them something to eat before they left home. She bought some snacks and drinks for the bus ride at the bus station, but not enough for the entire journey. She'd be able to buy a few small meals and snacks with the money

Adam had given her, but she felt that she'd have to be careful to make it last.

The bus had left in the early evening, and it was getting dark outside already. Brooke thought it would be a good idea to get the boys to sleep as soon as possible. She did not bring any pillows, but she had thought to bring two small lap blankets. The two older boys, Larry and Brian, shared one blanket, and Brooke and the youngest, Cecil, shared the other. Brooke made sure that Cecil had more of the blanket to help keep him warm.

It must have been the motion of the bus, but the boys had fallen asleep shortly after the bus left the station. Brooke wanted to sleep, but too many thoughts filled her head about what was happening and what might happen soon. She just stared out the window into the darkening night. After a while, Brooke just sighed, resigned herself to God's will, and trusted that He had a plan for her.

Early the next morning, as a sliver of light started showing in the sky over the horizon, Brooke woke up with a start. She looked around, trying to figure out where she was. The realization soon set in, and she realized she was on the bus with the boys. Brooke checked on Cecil, and he was sound asleep, leaning against the window. She looked up in front of her to see the two older boys awake.

"How long have you two been awake?" Brooke asked.

"We've been awake for a while," Larry said.

"Why didn't you wake me?"

"You looked tired. We didn't want to bother you," Brian added.

"Do you boys need to go to the bathroom?"

"No. Already taken care of," Larry said.

"Me, too," followed Brian.

After Cecil woke up and took care of business in the bathroom at the back of the bus, Brooke shared some snacks with them. She figured out they were already well into Oregon and would be in Spokane later that evening.

At lunchtime, the bus stopped at a diner just off the highway. All the passengers got off the bus to eat and stretch their legs. Brooke ordered food for all of them and then made a phone call while her sons remained in the booth inside the restaurant.

She found the phone booth outside the diner, put in her coins, and dialed her aunt's number. "Hello, aunt Gwen? This is Brooke."

"Well, hello, Brooke. How are you doing?" Gwen replied.

"I'm okay, but Adam put me and the boys on a bus to come up to Idaho. He said he was going to sell the house and move up when he was done."

There were a few moments of silence on the other end of the line. Then Gwen spoke. "Where is the bus coming into?"

"It's arriving in Spokane later this evening. Can you come to get us?" Brooke told her what time it was coming in.

"I don't feel comfortable driving in the dark. I could

get Val to go pick you up." Brooke was okay with that, and she would like to see her cousin again. Especially now.

Later that evening, after a long and tiring trip, the bus pulled into the terminal in downtown Spokane. Brooke and the boys were tired of sitting all that time. She knew her sons were eager to get off the bus. Brooke grabbed their suitcases with Larry's help and walked into the terminal. She looked around to see if her cousin Val was there. Brooke could not see her.

That was okay, since the bus had arrived at the terminal a few minutes early. Brooke found a spot for her and the boys to sit down where they could see the entrance to the bus terminal. It was only a few minutes before she heard her name.

"Brooke!"

She looked over and saw Val walking towards her. Val did not ask how her trip was or how the boys were. Gwen had filled her in earlier, and she knew what Brooke had been through in her life before this. Val walked straight towards Brooke and gave her a big hug. She held on to Val and quietly sobbed.

Once she finished hugging Brooke, Val moved over and hugged all three boys at once. "Good to see you again, kiddos." The boys all replied in kind.

Val looked at Brook while holding on to the boys and said, "Let's get you to mom's house."

Shelly was crying. She had a bundle of tissue in her hand, wiping her eyes and nose.

Sobbing, Shelly said, "Oh Brooke. I am so sorry you had to go through that. Jason and I were living in Indiana and we could have helped. I did not know."

"There wasn't anything you could have done," Brooke said in a comforting tone. "We were clear across the country from you and Jason."

"We were living in a large house with a swimming pool. Jason had a good job. We could have sent bus tickets for you and the boys to go out to Fort Wayne. We had the room," Shelly said.

"Shelly, it all worked out in the end. I do believe that God watched out for us."

Liz and Shelly nodded in agreement.

Brooke turned to Liz and asked, "Liz, do you remember when Adam talked you and Kevin into riding in the motorhome up here to Idaho?"

"How could I forget? Kevin and I were just married. We didn't have a lot of money, and one day Adam asked us if we could ride in the motorhome with him up to Idaho. He said he would then send us back to California on a bus. We both thought, Sure, what the hell? It sounded like a neat little adventure. Once we got up there, Adam refused to buy our tickets, and we thought we were going to be stranded. We didn't have the money to get back home. Then Adam told Kevin and me to go ahead and drive the motorhome back and take it to the address that he gave us."

"I didn't know any of this, Liz," Brooke exclaimed.

"I'm not surprised," said Liz. "He wasn't even going to

give us money for gas, and we told him we didn't have close to enough to get us home. So he gave us about $70 in traveler's checks. We left right after we got the money. Kevin had to get back to work. It was tight. We barely ate anything on the trip back. Well, to finish up the story, we ran out of gas and money about ten miles from home. We stood on the side of the road for a little while, trying to figure out what we should do. Cell phones, of course, didn't exist at the time. Then one of Kevin's dad's coworkers recognized us while we stood outside the motorhome. He stopped and told us he would go get us some gas. We really lucked out. Well, we returned the motorhome back to the location Adam gave us. That was when we figured out he didn't actually buy the motorhome but was test driving it for a little while."

Liz's story seemed to stop Shelly from crying, and she even got a little laugh from her.

"That sounds like quite the adventure and makes for a good story, doesn't it?" Shelly said. Liz nodded.

Brooke looked at the clock. "Hey! How about we stop for lunch?"

BROOKE- THE CONCLUSION

Shelly, Brooke, and Liz returned to the living room after a filling lunch. The ladies needed a much deserved emotional break. They sat down in their usual seats and got comfortable.

"Now, where were we?" Brooke wondered.

"I had told you about Kevin and me riding up with Adam in the motorhome. What happened after we left?" Liz said as she leaned forward a bit in her chair.

"Well, we were able to rent a small home by the river and lived there for a little while. Adam found a job in Spokane, so he had a long drive to work and back. I think it was around forty-five to fifty minutes each way. Later, he found property in the country that had a single wide mobile home on it. We bought it with a little money we saved from his job."

"That was the property just down the road from where Jason and I lived, right? Shelly mentioned.

"Yes. That's right. But it wasn't quite like how you remembered it."

Shelly and Jason had moved to Idaho from Indiana in the early 1980s. Shelly wanted to be near her sister and other relatives for a change. They were able to buy a nice double wide home on five acres of land about three miles away from Brooke and Adam.

"Well, we found out later that the trailer on the property didn't come with and it wasn't part of the deal. Shortly after we moved in and got settled down, the owners came back and told us we needed to get out. The previous owners wanted to move it out to a different place."

" Did you let them?" Liz asked.

"Well, they provided the paperwork, and we saw we had to move our stuff out. Fortunately, we didn't have a lot of things since we had just recently moved there. Adam was able to get a hold of an old school bus that a friend of his had. Someone already ripped the seats out, and the only thing on the bus was a small old wood stove with a pipe that rose through the roof. Whoever put the stove in did a good job of sealing the pipe and roof. Well, we had no other choice but to store some of our things and then move what we could into the bus."

"Since the bus didn't have any beds or cots, we

drove to the Army/Navy surplus store and found some old metal bunks with some mattresses. Adam and I put some in the back for the boys and pushed another two beds together near the front of the bus for Adam and me. The stove provided enough heat during winter, but it was still on the cool side at times."

"What did you do for cooking?" Shelly asked.

"We formed a little table for the kitchen and used a little two-burner camp stove. Since there wasn't any running water, we had to go get it from town and carry it onto the bus."

The area where Brooke and Adam lived was newly developed. A well had not been dug by the previous owners for their mobile home. They realized that the other owners must have carted their water in as well. Even during winter.

"How long did you live on that bus?" Liz asked

"About two winters."

Shelly started crying, feeling guilty that she didn't help her sister. "I didn't know, Brooke! I wish you would have called me to help you. Jason and I could've sent you some money. I wasn't even a good big sister to you." Shelly continued crying. Her guilt still strong after all these decades.

"I never really thought of it. We were just trying to get by," Brooke replied.

Liz chimed in, "I just thought of something. How did you go to the bathroom? I don't think there was one on the bus, was there?"

"No. Not on the bus, but there was an outhouse on the property. It wasn't much fun to use. The outhouse was freezing in the winter and stinking in the summer. We only used it when it was absolutely necessary. Aunt Gwen let us shower at her place. I think we drove over there maybe twice a week. The other times we just used some water heated up on the camp stove and a washcloth and cleaned up a bit inside the bus. Whenever we drove to the store or Aunt Gwen's, we took advantage and used the toilet. The boys used the restrooms in the school, and they would shower after gym class, which helped a lot."

"Did the boys have fun? Was it like camping to them?" Liz asked.

"No, I could tell it embarrassed them. We didn't have much money and had to buy their clothes at the thrift store. Back then, thrift stores didn't stock quality clothes like they do now."

Brooke and Adam's three boys handled it as well as expected. It was tough on them. The clothes they had to wear were always a little too big and never fashionable. As school students, fitting in with others seemed to carry more importance than it should have. The boys made the best of their situation and learned from it.

"After a year or so, Adam and the kids built a large lean-to with a loft in it. The boys slept in the loft while Adam and I slept on the bus. They liked the loft, but they didn't like the bus," Brooke said.

"When did you get the mobile home?" Shelly asked.

"Not long before you and Jason moved out here from Fort Wayne, Adam had hurt his back at his job and got a nice settlement. He took that money and bought the mobile home. Living on a bus for two years and then moving into the trailer was like moving into a mansion for us."

"I had to start working to make some money since Adam got hurt. With the money running low, I began cutting trees and making fence posts to sell with a neighbor lady who I had become friends with. Adam never helped me. He always laid on the couch and claimed he was too much in pain to help. I wasn't convinced and thought he should've helped. Anything! But he didn't."

"Why am I not surprised?" Liz said with a chuckle.

Prior to getting injured Adam would include his sons on little building projects around their property. Cutting firewood for the winter was a top priority. He taught the two older boys, Larry and Brian, the safe way to swing an ax. At one point Adam and the boys built a livestock pen with trees they cut down on their land. Living out in the country provided a good opportunity for Adam and the boys to go hunting and fishing to help supplement the food.

"Adam never worked after the injury, so I had to go out and get a job, since selling fence posts didn't provide enough. I found one at a resort nearby and started working as a housekeeper. Finally, we had a steady income. As fate would have it, after working there for a while, I hurt my back and couldn't work for about nine months.

Keep in mind that Adam didn't work, so times were hard then. There was some unemployment compensation and some money that I saved while working, but we needed to stretch it out."

Liz just shook her head in disbelief. "Kevin had a decent job at the time, and we had little money saved up, but we could've sent some to you."

"Jason and I could have sent some as well. Jason was a manager at a pizza place, and we had more than enough money," Shelly added.

"I didn't even think about that. Every morning I prayed to God to give me the strength and guidance to get through this, and I had faith that he would provide. That didn't last very long, though. Something that Adam said one day just broke me."

Liz and Shelly said nothing after Brooke's comment. They could see in her eyes that the comment made so many years ago still bothered her to this day. Shelly and Liz waited patiently for Brooke to gather her thoughts and begin the story of what Adam had said to her that still makes her emotional.

"Adam had gotten mad at Brian for something and told him he's nothing but a slob like his mom. I was standing off to the side in the same room. Adam's comment hit me hard, and I became emotionally dead in that instant. A numb feeling came over me. I lost all love and concern for anything and anyone around me and stopped being there for my boys."

"That sounds sort of like the way Bill treated me, but we'll talk about that later." Shelly said.

"Not long afterward, I got a call from the resort. The office asked me if I wanted to come back to work. Not as a housekeeper, but in the sales department. I must have impressed them while I was there before, so I started back to work as a closer in sales. That is where I met Mark. He was in sales and helped me along on the job. We started becoming friends, and I liked his company. Mark made me feel like I was smart and always encouraged me. I started loving the hours at work and spent more time away from home. I had neglected the boys and the home. All my time away had consequences. None of the boys graduated from high school. Instead, they all dropped out, and all three had gotten girls pregnant by the time they were sixteen years old. To this day, I still feel guilty about that. But thanks to God's forgiveness and that program I've been doing through the church, I could forgive myself."

"That's the program you're using to help Mom, right?" Liz asked.

"Right," Brooke replied.

"I can see how well it's been working for you. I mean, you look so happy and content," Liz complimented Brook.

"There are quite a few steps, and it takes a long time, but your mom only has a few weeks. So we are going through a sort of crash course for her. Before you got here, and since you've been here, we've been doing nothing but going over our past. We're finding out where the problems began and how we failed to deal with them," Brooke said.

"Guess we still have several of the things to talk about regarding dad. That's going to take at least a full day or longer. All the things he did to us and especially to mom." Liz said. "Anyway, let's finish up with your story and how you got through this."

Brooke agreed and continued, "Things started going even better at work. Mark and I would sometimes meet for lunch and talk about many things. We talked about life, current events, family, and other things like that. The great way Mark treated me made me realize just how bad things were with Adam and that I wasn't being treated how I should have been. Adam hadn't worked in a long time, and so I had to do something to help him. I was determined to make this marriage work. So I convinced him to study for and take the real estate test to get his license. I figured he might make a good salesman."

Liz interrupted. "Adam talked Kevin and me into going up to Idaho in a motorhome with very little money. He should have been a natural at sales."

"You would think." Brooke replied. "After he got his license, I got him a mobile phone. This was several years ago, and those things were like bricks back then. I asked him for the phone number since he had to start the service, and he told me he wasn't giving me the number. It's for work. I was suspicious before about his having affairs with women. Adam cheated on me in California, so why wouldn't he cheat on me up in Idaho?

One day, I just realized I couldn't take it anymore. God was telling me to move on, and I told Adam I wanted to talk. So we sat down on the bed in our bedroom and I told him I couldn't do this anymore. The cell phone number was the last straw. He treated me bad throughout our marriage. He cheated on me on different occasions. I just couldn't take it anymore. It was time to separate. So he moved out, and since his parents moved back up to Idaho, he went to live with them for a while until he found a place of his own."

"I know you stayed in the mobile home for a while," Shelly recalled.

"Yes, that's right." Brooke replied.

"I just thought of something. Adam and you were still together when dad stayed with us because of his emphysema, right?" Shelly said.

Brooke told Shelly she remembered some of it. During that time, Brooke and Adam were going through tough times, trying to make ends meet.

"It was not a good time for us or for dad. The emphysema ate him down so much that he looked like a skeleton. Dad was always thin to begin with."

Brooke replied, "I wish I had spent more time with him during his sickness. We had our own problems, and things were a little difficult."

"Brooke, I understand. It was hard for me to watch dad wither away like that. He got so bad that he couldn't control his bodily functions and had to wear diapers. When he got too weak to change his own diapers, Jason stepped up and did it. There was no way I could change his diapers. Not on our own dad."

"I went to see him when he was in the hospital," Brooke said. "The nurse had said they didn't expect him to live much longer. I visited with him a little and then left. I kissed him on the cheek and told him I loved him very much. Something in my gut told me this was the last time I would see him alive. When I got back home, Adam said the hospital called, and he had just passed away."

Shelly replied, "I will never forget getting that phone call. I knew it was coming soon."

Before dad went to the hospital, he was in bed at Shelly and Jason's house. Jason had just changed Jake's diaper. A task that is difficult enough to do but for a grown man to have it done on him must be humiliating. After Jason cleaned up and threw away the diaper he sat down on the side of the bed and he and Jake had a heart-to-heart talk. Jake suddenly got peaceful, almost serene. He told Jason what a good man he was and a good husband he was to Shelly. He then told Jason to make sure to take good care of me. Jason told Shelly this story a little later and it was something neither Jason nor Shelly would ever forget.

Shelly and Brooke's father, Jake Gallagher, died in 1984. He had a small funeral with his sisters and other relatives in attendance. Jake's headstone was basic.

Etched into the stone, other than the usual information, was a pair of cowboy boots in one corner. Jake was a lifelong, true-blue cowboy.

"I'm sorry, Brooke, we got sidetracked a bit."

"That's okay. It was nice thinking about dad for a little while. Anyway, I continued to work at the resort for about ten years before I got that job at the local newspaper. They had offered me an excellent position. I remained friends with Mark, but I started to develop feelings for him and wanted to be more than friends. Unfortunately, he was married at the time. Well! About three years had passed. We continued to stay in touch with each other from time to time, and I got a call from him one day. It was different from other calls from him over those three years. He asked if I wanted to go out on a date. I was surprised. I asked about his wife and reminded him he was married. He said he wasn't, and that they had gotten a divorce. I was doubtful, but I was hoping it was true. He said he got divorced and wanted to prove it. He knew my fax number at the newspaper office, so he sent me a news clipping of his ex wife's wedding announcement to another man."

"She didn't waste any time finding another husband, did she?" Liz exclaimed.

"No, she didn't. I couldn't believe how fast that was. I was divorced, and he was divorced. God was answering my prayers. We started going out and becoming serious. One day, about four months later, he asked me to marry him. It was like a fairy tale to me. Of course, I said yes.

That part was great. But there was still something else weighing heavily on me."

"I can't see what it could have been. You had a good husband. You had a good job," Liz remarked.

"Do you recall when I told you about shutting down emotionally and not being there for my kids? Well, that part hadn't really changed. Larry had four kids with his first wife, and since she was using drugs, her mind was not right. Eventually, she wanted nothing to do with Larry or the kids, so she left them. I still feel guilty today for burying myself in my work and not being there for him and the grandkids. That is something I'm overcoming now. I keep asking God for forgiveness, and all that I have been able to forgive myself for, this is the one thing I still haven't come to terms with to this day." Brooke said, while starting to cry.

Shelly and Liz both got up and hugged Brooke in a warm embrace.

"Look at how the boys turned out now. You have great grandkids, and Larry and Cecil are doing great in their careers. I know Brian would have been doing well today," Shelly said.

Brooke's middle son, Brian, died several years ago in a motorcycle accident. His teens and early twenties were hard times for him. Later, Brian settled down, married a good woman, and had a son and a daughter.

"When did you and Mark start having trouble? I know you said things were like a fairy tale for a long time," Shelly asked.

"Mark retired around 2009. He drank socially before his retirement. We both enjoyed a glass of wine or beer at times. But he started drinking heavier. Soon he started on hard liquor. That was when his mood started to change. He got a little more moody and would get upset at the littlest things. One day, I told him to get some help with his drinking. He tried, but it was like he didn't want to change. The worst part was that he was messing around on me. I thought maybe it was because of his drinking. This went on for several years. He would go to therapy now and then just to keep me happy, but I couldn't take it any longer. Seeing that he wasn't interested in getting any help, I divorced him."

"How are you doing now? Emotionally, that is?" Liz asked.

"Liz, I'm doing great. I am happy, and most of all, I am content. Not only am I content with myself, but I'm content with God. I hope you understand what I mean."

"I think I do," Liz replied as she nodded.

"Don't take this the wrong way, Liz, but I sometimes envy what you and Kevin have in your marriage. Don't get me wrong. I am so happy you have a great relationship, but I sometimes wish I could have had that in a husband. You, Jesse, Gary, and Melanie have such wonderful spouses. I am so proud of all of you."

"Thank you, Aunt Brooke," Liz replied as she smiled.

Shelly added as she looked at Liz, "Don't I know it! I have wonderful kids and wonderful in-laws."

SHELLY AND BILL- PART 1

Liz compared Shelly and Brookes' sides of the family. They compared each other's challenges and obstacles that happened at different times, as well as their own difficulties.

"We moved over twenty times when I was a little kid," Liz said. "At least we never had to live on a school bus, so you got us on that one." The ladies all chuckled.

Liz has the gift of knowing when a little humor is needed in situations. She can make anyone feel at ease.

"In fact, we moved so many times in Spokane alone, when you and Jesse were born. I don't understand why, but I suspected Bill would move us into a place and then never pay rent," Shelly said.

"Well, I'm not surprised. Look at all the things he did to us," Liz added.

"There is one thing he did to me that I have never told anyone. If I'm going to have any chance of getting out of this depression that I always find myself in, and with the help of Brooke's program from the church, I figure I should share this."

"What is it? From all we talked about, I thought everything had been said when it came to dad."

"Well! It was back during the gathering after Mom's funeral. We were back at dad's house and it devastated him after Mom shot herself. Bill and I had just gotten married not long before the funeral."

December 1956 in Sandpoint, Idaho. The day was bitter. They had laid Marilyn Gallagher to rest. Marilyn ended her own life at the barrel of a gun. The family was grief stricken, but they weren't completely surprised. Marilyn had attempted to kill herself before when she tried to hang herself in the attic. Her husband, Jake, had found her in time.

Marilyn battled depression for most of her married life and wanted out of her marriage to Jake for a long time. She had a chance to follow a man to New York she was infatuated with. But her parents kept his letters to her a secret and never told her about the man wanting to take her to New York. They wanted her to stay since she already had a family.

The death of her son, Stevie, from cancer, hit her hard. She couldn't deal with life anymore.

At the gathering after her funeral, Jake sat quietly in his favorite chair inside his house. He said little except to say 'thank you' and give a slight smile when people expressed their condolences to him.

Ten-year-old Brooke, Jake and Marilyn's youngest daughter, wandered around the house. She tried to stay away from the well-meaning hugs and pats on the head from relatives who were expressing their sorrow. Brooke understood they meant well, but it just made her feel uncomfortable. She could not process her mother's death at this young age. Brooke just pranced around giggling and playing with other kids. The house was not big and she couldn't quite hide very well. So she just accepted the fact that she was to be on the receiving end of the family's affections and often touchy condolences.

Sixteen-year-old Shelly, Jake and Marilyn's oldest daughter, was there at the house with her new husband, Bill. Shelly, too, was on the receiving end of many tearful hugs and well wishes.

After a while, Bill whispered in Shelly's ear.

"Shelly, come with me to the bathroom. I want to talk to you," Bill said.

Bill and Shelly walked through the crowd of mourners that filled the room. The bathroom was towards the back of the house, away from the people in the home. Shelly walked into the bathroom, followed by Bill. He turned, shut the door, and locked it.

"What did you want to talk about?"

Bill did not answer her, but walked over to Shelly and

grabbed her by the shoulders. He shoved her up against the sink. Not hard, but just enough to move her.

"What are you doing?" Shelly asked in a quiet voice, just above a whisper.

"Shut up." Bill kept his voice low so he would not arouse suspicion from the people outside the bathroom.

He forced himself on Shelly. She didn't know what to think. Bill was her husband, but this was not right. Not during a time like this, just after her mother died and during the mourning. Why was he doing this?

Shelly didn't want to continue and pleaded with Bill to stop.

"Bill! Please stop," she said, crying and sobbing. "Please don't do this. It isn't right."

Bill said nothing while he kept forcing himself on her. Shelly wanted to cry out. There were uncles and cousins in the house who would have rushed in to help if she called out. She kept silent, though. Shelly didn't want to ruin what was going on outside. Her dad was in pain and grieving. She didn't want to add to it.

Once Bill finished, he pulled up his pants and made sure his hair was in place.

Calmly and unfazed by what had just happened, Bill looked over at Shelly.

"Get dressed and pull yourself together." Bill cracked the door and checked to see if anyone was on the other side.

As he walked out the door and closed it, Bill never looked back at Shelly to check if she was okay. She stood alone in the bathroom. Tears streamed down her face. Shelly felt small and worthless, and she wondered how Bill could do something like this to her.

Shelly wiped the tears from her face and fastened her clothes back up. She checked her hair in the mirror. After finishing getting dressed, she stepped in front of the bathroom door and stood there for a few moments. Shelly tried getting up the courage to face the crowd in the main part of the house. Would they somehow suspect something happened? Would they suspect something was wrong?

Shelly took a deep breath and opened the door. People were talking out in the kitchen and living room, just like they were talking when she walked into the bathroom. Heading out to where the people were, Shelly walked among them, trying to see if anyone looked at her differently. She received more condolences for her mother. No different from before.

Shelly walked near Bill while he was talking with a few of Shelly's relatives. He pulled her close, wrapped one arm around her waist, and asked, "How are you doing, honey?"

"I'm ok." That was all Shelly could say.

Bill acted as if nothing had happened. How could he behave that way? Shelly could not understand how Bill could stand there, as if he had not forced himself on her in the bathroom a few minutes earlier.

Shelly wiped the tears from her eyes as she finished

telling Liz and Brooke the story. Both of them were also wiping away the tears with tissues.

"Mom, I am so sorry that happened to you. Why didn't you tell me this before? He raped you, mom. It doesn't matter that you guys were married," Liz said. "Why didn't you call out for help?"

"At the time, I didn't want to cause a problem or upset people given what everyone was there for," Shelly answered.

"I think I can understand," Liz said.

"This was how Jesse was conceived. I wanted to leave Bill, but Brooke, I had similar thoughts you had that I may never have another chance to find love, so I stayed with him."

"It's a bad feeling, like being too vulnerable," Brooke replied.

"Yes, it is. Bill made me feel low and unimportant for what he did to me that day. It wasn't the last time he made me feel like dirt. One time was when we were living in Spokane in a little apartment on the second floor. I don't remember the exact day it happened. Bill and I lived in so many places around Spokane that it's hard to remember the exact location of the place. We lived in close to twenty-two different places in that same city during the time both Jesse and Liz were born. I didn't think about it then, but now that I think about it, Bill probably never paid rent at any of them."

"Twenty-two different apartments? In what, two

years? We didn't even move that many times in our entire marriage," Brooke said.

"Boggles the mind, doesn't it? Anyway, one day, when I was pregnant with Jesse, I decided to make an enchilada casserole for the first time. I had gotten the recipe and wanted to impress him. I knew when he would get home from work, so I wanted to have dinner ready for him. When he got home, he gave me a kiss and changed his clothes. I was sure he would notice the aroma of the enchilada casserole, but he said nothing about it."

"How can you not notice it? I bet it was excellent," Liz said.

"Yes, it sure was," Shelly said.

"Oh my God! Those casseroles you made were always delicious. I noticed the smell of those being made even when I played outside," Liz reminisced.

"Well, he came in and sat down at the little wooden table in the middle of the small kitchen. So I sat down near him since I already set the table and put the casserole on the hot pad. I cut the casserole into slices, dishing his up, and then putting a slice on my plate. I thought for sure he was going to like it."

"Jesse, Gary, and I always liked it. It was one of our favorite dishes when we were kids," Liz said.

"Bill cut out a piece of the casserole with his fork and took a bite. I sat there, waiting for him to tell me how good it was. I hadn't even started eating. Just as he ate the first bite, instead of telling me he liked it, he looked at me and asked what kind of crap it was. Well, Bill used harsher words that I won't repeat now. If he had just said those words and left it at that, I would have been okay. Moving his chair back a little, Bill lifted his leg and kicked me in the side near my waist. If I recall, it was like a cross between a kick and a hard shove. I flew off the chair and landed on the floor near the sink."

"You said you were pregnant with Jesse, right?" Brooked asked.

"Yes. I was about six or seven months pregnant. I looked up from the floor at Bill, and he just stared at me with a look of disgust. He shook his head a little and left the apartment. I don't know where he went, but I kept thinking that it was somehow my fault and that I should have done better." Shelly said.

"Makes me hate him even more," Liz said. "We've barely scratched the surface of what all he did to you and us kids."

"You don't still think it was your fault, do you?" Brooke asked.

"Oh no. Not at all." Shelly replied. "I know it wasn't my fault now, but I'm not sure if I ever got over being made to feel like crap and treated that way."

"Part of me wants to say that you should have left that jerk. But the other part of me knows that if you left him after that, neither Gary nor I would have been born. You would have been without your favorite child," Liz said.

"Gary, right?" Shelly said, and the ladies all chuckled.

After the laughter died down, Liz leaned over and said

teasingly, "I meant me. You know, your favorite! Wink, wink."

That brought a bigger laugh to all three women. It helped to ease Shelly's tensions and emotional state a bit after she told Brooke and Liz a few things about her traumatic experiences with Bill.

"One reason I may have stayed with him was that there were good times, too. There was a fair amount of traveling, and we got to see a lot of neat places."

Shelly just remembered something about her past that she had long since forgotten. There was a trip she took on a train with Jesse and Liz when they were little.

"The talk about traveling jogged my memory. I said I had always wanted to ride the train? That it was on my bucket list?"

Both Liz and Brooke replied they remembered.

"Well, I actually rode a train from Fort Wayne out to Sandpoint in Idaho when I was about eighteen or nineteen. Liz, you were around 6 months old and in diapers, and Jesse was just over a year and a half."

"Obviously, I don't remember that," Liz joked. "Where was dad?"

Shelly told the story that led up to her taking the train with Jesse and Liz.

"After your dad got out of the military, we moved back to Indiana and lived with his mom for a little while. Bill had told me that grandma Jorgensen owned a big restaurant. It turns out she had some small tables set up in her front room and dining area and served home-cooked meals to the factory workers during their lunchtime. I helped your grandma with the cooking and serving. The men who came to eat always loved the food she cooked. They also looked forward just as much to her homemade pies."

"Grandma's cooking, especially her homemade pumpkin pies, was so delicious. Thinking about her food is making my mouth water right now," Liz reminisced. Besides the homemade pumpkin pies, grandma Jorgensen's homemade rolls were the talk of the town. She made the rolls from scratch and no matter how close others would follow her recipe, they could never match her rolls.

Shelly continued. "Yep! Her cooking was legendary in the area. The homemade rolls she made were heavenly. Anyway, I don't know the exact reasons or how we got to the train station, but I was escaping from your dad. I must have had at least a suitcase and a small bag because I had to carry diapers. Somehow, I paid for the ticket and I don't know where I got the money for food or what I fed you and Jesse, but we somehow made the two-day trip."

"I think I understand why you forgot it or didn't count that train trip. It sounded like it was rather traumatic and you couldn't enjoy it. Not like your train trip out here this time," Brooke said.

"Well, I called aunt Gwen to pick us up at the Sandpoint train station in the middle of the night when the train got in. The kids and I ended up staying with aunt

Irene and uncle Lee for a little while. One day, they got a letter that was addressed to me, and it was from Bill. He said he was driving out to get us and bring us back, and if I didn't go back with him, he was going to shoot himself.

Another day or two later, uncle Lee, who was a cop in the town, suddenly left the house. He didn't tell us why he left. Uncle Lee came back a little later and said he had gotten word that Bill was in town. He left the house to intercept Bill and searched him and his car, but he didn't find any guns."

"Do you know why you took him back?" Liz asked, "It must have been hard for you, but I bet Gary would be thankful. He didn't come along until later."

Both Shelly and Brooke chuckled.

"I understand. But the funny thing is that I don't even know why I got back with him after all the things he had done to me. We moved back to Indiana for a while, but then later we moved to California. That was where your dad got a job working on the dam and where Gary was born." Shelly recalled.

"I remember some of that time when Gary came along and that I had a baby brother to torment," Liz said jokingly.

The three ladies all laughed. Gary most likely would have laughed as well. Liz and Gary always got along well, aside from the occasional fight as little kids.

"Later on, we moved back to Indiana for a little while

when Gary was just a toddler. Then we moved back out west to the Tacoma area," Shelly said.

"Mom, didn't we live in three different places out there? One place I remember was a small apartment complex. That was the one we could see Mt. Rainier from the parking lot," Liz said.

"Yes, I remember that place," Shelly replied.

"I don't think we were there very long. After that apartment, we moved to the house with the tall pine tree that Jesse used to climb," Liz reminisced.

"There is a picture we have of Jesse standing at the top of that tree. It scared me half to death," Shelly said.

"Do you remember the pictures of us in the backyard with the neighbor kids? Jumping off that swing, and the funniest one was burying Gary up to his neck with grass clippings while he sat in the wheelbarrow. I think he had as much fun in there as we did putting the grass on him." Liz reminisced.

"You kids sure had quite an eventful childhood. Both good and bad," Shelly said.

"That last house we moved to in western Washington had a lot of good and bad times. There were those woods next to the house, where we would walk to the stream and catch trout. Jesse, Gary, and I would bring the trout back to the house and put them in that little cement pond behind the house." Liz told.

"Those fish smelled awful and wouldn't last long at all. I had to clean up after you kids."

"Well, that's what moms are for," Liz replied.

Brooke had been quiet while Liz and Shelly were talking about their past, as she was fine to sit there and listen. She had already shared a lot of her past that neither Shelly nor Liz knew about. Now she was listening to stories she either knew nothing abut or knew little about.

"Do you remember that pool table Dad bought?"

"Yes. I don't know why Bill bought it when we could have used the money for other things." Shelly answered.

"We had as much fun with the big box it came in," Liz said.

"What did you all do with the box? Build a fort or something?" Brooke asked.

"No, we flattened it out, and in the winter, we used it as a giant sled down that hill in front of our house. The funny thing was that when we slid down, we would have to roll off and grab the cardboard to stop it. If we didn't, we would slide into the barbed wire fence that bordered the horse pasture below us," Liz said.

Shelly started laughing. "I think I know what's coming next. The barbed wire incident." The barbed wire story has been told repeatedly amongst the family. It has been a fond and funny remembrance for everyone, including Liz.

"More laughs at my expense." Liz rolled her eyes. "As I told you, aunt Brooke, we would have to roll off before we got the fence. Dad, Jesse, Gary, and I were all on the sled. Mom was standing at the top of the hill in front of the house, watching. One time, we got close to the fence and all the others rolled off. I was having so much fun that I forgot to roll off. Dad and the others were shouting, and by the time I realized what was happening, it was too late to roll off. At the last second, I turned onto my stomach and got flat, hoping I could go underneath."

"Did you make it?" Brooke asked.

"Nope. A barb from the fence caught me right on the seat of my pants."

Brooke and Shelly started laughing. Shelly still laughed at this story every time Liz told it.

"Did it cut you?" Brooke asked.

"No. I was lucky. Since it was winter and we dressed for the cold, it just the outer layer had ripped. We got to keep the box and went sledding on other days. I can tell you I learned my lesson and was one of the first ones to roll off." Liz said as they all continued to laugh.

"There were some good times there and I'm glad for those. Those times helped to lessen the pain of the bad times," Shelly said.

"Yep. There were good times. One time, Dad took Jesse, Gary, and I camping up into Canada."

"I remember that. Your dad and I were separated for a short while. We separated a lot, and I always took him back. Anyway, I packed clothes and food for you kids. I think I even packed some things for your dad." Shelly recalled it, but not fondly.

"Aunt Brooke, I don't think we ever told you about our camping trip up there into Canada. It was definitely one to remember." Liz said.

"No. I never heard about it. What happened?" Brooke asked.

"Dad had borrowed a pop-up camper from one of his friends, and we drove up to Canada. I don't know where we traveled to, but the towns we passed through were tiny. I'm not even sure if he had a place in mind or was just driving until we found a spot that looked promising. The place we settled on was next to a clear mountain river on top of a bank. The air smelled so fresh that it stopped you in your tracks."

"I've been to places like that. I know what you mean," Brooke added.

Liz and Shelly both shook their heads in agreement. The Pacific Northwest had places like that all over. The small rivers were crystal clear and the air so fresh that it felt like one breath could clean out your entire system.

Liz continued, "We helped dad set up the camper and get the food ready. After that, we just played around and had fun. We brought a BB gun we borrowed from the neighbors, and Gary was using it near the edge of the river, up on the bank. It was about a two- or three-foot drop into the water. He was messing around when he dropped the BB gun into the water. Dad saw it happen, and he yelled at him. The look on his face when dad yelled at him made me sad for Gary. We couldn't see the bottom because the river was flowing fast. Dad told me to come with him to the edge. He told me to get over by the edge of the bank, and he held my ankles as he lowered me into the water. Dad dunked me head first,

I might add, into the cold water at the spot where Gary dropped the gun."

Shelly spoke up. "When I learned about that after the trip, I was furious with Bill. I know that water must have been freezing."

"It was. I couldn't see anything because of how fast the water was moving. I was using my hands to search the bottom. Dad would pull me up and try another spot. We gave up after several minutes of trying. Besides the water being cold, I actually had fun. I don't think Gary had much fun when he woke up in the camper the next morning and said the side of his face hurt. We all looked at him, and I think our mouths dropped. One side of his face was lumpy. He had somehow gotten the mumps. Dad told us the trip was over, and so we packed up and left. Gary told me later that he did have fun on that trip despite getting the mumps and dropping the BB gun."

"There were a fair amount of bad times as well," Liz replied. "Like when dad cheated on you and had another girlfriend."

"Her name was Lily. I know she had a daughter and a son, but I never knew their names," Shelly said.

"I found out about Lily in an interesting way. Dad said he wanted to take me to the Glen Campbell concert. I was excited to see him perform. It was going to be like father-daughter time. We got there, and he introduced me to a woman he said was a friend and said I might get along with her daughter. Her son was too young, so she must have left him with a babysitter. I didn't think much of it since I was only in the third or fourth grade. Then it got a little weird. I was sitting on one side of dad, and Lily was on the other, with her daughter on the far side. I looked down and saw him holding her hand." Liz said.

"That must have been weird for you. Did you say anything or do anything?" Brooke asked.

"No. I just sat there and listened to the concert. I felt pretty uncomfortable for the rest of the show."

"Shelly, did you suspect anything?" Brooke asked, looking over at her sister.

"I started to a little later. Once I discovered he was seeing someone, I found out who it was, and I called her. When she answered, I told her who I was and said that I was Bill's wife and we had three kids. I told her how long we had been married."

"How did she react?" Brooke asked, knowing beforehand that Bill had an affair but never really learning the details about it.

"At first, she didn't believe me. The call didn't go on for much longer. She hung up soon after that. I tried again, and she was convinced that Bill was going to leave us for her."

"One day, I got the idea of having her come over during dinner. I called her up and told her I could prove Bill was staying with us. I asked her if she would come over during our meal. She said she would."

"That doesn't sound good. How did it go? There wasn't any fighting, was there?" Brooke asked.

"No. The kids had gone with their grandma, but I

don't remember where. I had just put the spaghetti on the table and sat down when I saw her car drive up the lane. Bill's back was to the lane, so he couldn't see the car coming. I got up and opened the door, and Lily walked in. Bill's face got red. I could tell he was both embarrassed and pissed. Lily looked at him and told him to choose between us. Bill kind of mixed up his words a bit, but then said he was choosing me and the kids. Lily didn't start crying. She just had an upset look on her face and turned and left, saying nothing."

"How did Bill react after that?" Brooke asked.

"Neither of us talked afterward. Bill ate his dinner without saying anything and then went into his office and shut the door. Later on, I heard him talking on the phone, so I walked out of the kitchen and then stood outside the door to his little office and listened. He was talking to Lily. I heard him tell her he was really protecting her from me and that he chose her. Bill also told her he was trying to get me committed to a mental hospital for my own good. He told her I was dangerous to myself and others. That was all I needed to hear, so I charged into the room and started yelling at him. I don't remember exactly what I said, but I was angry and hurt."

"How you could stay with him after that," Liz said.

"I know, but I had you kids to think about."

"I really hated how dad treated you and the abuse you took from him. One time when grandma Jorgensen was staying with us. Dad got mad at you for some reason, and he had you against the wall and was ramming the back of your head into it. Grandma came up to stop it, and dad looked right at her and told her to get back downstairs. He didn't even shout it. That's what made it scary. Dad was yelling at you, mom, but then he spoke to grandma in that lower but equally terrifying voice," Liz said.

"I don't remember that," Shelly replied.

Liz told Shelly and Brooke about an incident Gary told her of when they lived in that same house.

Late one evening, Gary was sleeping in his room and awoke to loud noises coming from outside his door. He got up from his bed, still sleepy, and walked over to the door. Gary heard yelling outside in the hallway. He turned the door knob and opened the door enough to peek out, afraid of the shouting.

Gary saw his father grabbing his mother by the hair, a handful in each hand on the sides of her head. Bill was ramming Shelly's head into the wall he had forced her against, shouting at her. Gary couldn't remember what was being said. He was only six years old.

What he remembers most about that moment was his mother's face. Her hands were up near her face and were shaking from fear. She was crying hysterically and pleading for him to stop. Gary was just a little boy and felt he could do nothing. He shut the door gently, then turned and ran back to his bed and buried himself under the covers. He didn't cry, but just laid under the covers until he fell asleep.

"That doesn't ring a bell, either. Maybe my mind had blocked out those horrible times."

"Gary said he woke up the next morning and dad acted as if nothing had happened. Talk about a real psycho." Liz said.

"Was that the last of Lily? What ended up happening?" Brooke asked.

Getting hungry after talking for a long time, Shelly suggested they break for lunch. "Let's get some lunch, and I'll tell you more about that part and when we moved down to Las Vegas."

SHELLY AND BILL- PART 2

Brooke, Shelly, and Liz ate lunch at a nearby Chinese buffet. The restaurant served decent food, and it was easy to converse with each other. The conversation was light, and they talked about their kids and grandchildren through most of the meal. It was a refreshing break from the discussions about Shelly and Brooke's troubled past.

Once they returned home and settled into their chairs, Shelly started the conversation. "I think I was getting ready to tell you about Bill moving us to Las Vegas. We packed everything up and used a moving trailer to move everything down there. Bill found us a tiny house to live in. Once we settled in, I enrolled the kids in a school close to the house."

"I was in the fourth grade, Jesse in fifth, and Gary in

first grade, and I'm pretty sure he doesn't recall much about that school. The only thing he told me about that school was being outside for lunch and you bringing him food from a fast-food restaurant. Not much had happened there for us. I remember the streets were so hot you couldn't walk on them barefooted." Liz recalled.

"That dry heat was terrible. It felt as though my skin would shrivel up from how dry it was. I also remember that your dad bought Jesse that little rifle for a present," Shelly added.

"Yep. It was a .22 rifle with a scope and I bet Jesse still has that rifle to this day," Liz said. "Dad had taken us out into the desert for target practice. We still have photos from that day."

Jesse kept the rifle well into his adult life. He hunted with it when he was young and let Liz and Gary shoot several rounds through it. Later on, Jesse gave the rifle to one of his grandkids. Well, perhaps loaned it would be a better choice of words. Jesse is still very attached to that rifle for nostalgic reasons.

"I was mad at Bill for buying him a gun. Jesse was too young." Brooke nodded in agreement, but Liz shrugged a bit. She was not sure if it was that bad of an idea.

"Liz, you don't think it was a bad idea?" Brooke asked.

"Not really. Nothing bad happened. Dad showed Jesse and me how to use it and how to aim it. Gary was way too young, so he just played in the sand."

Brooke and Shelly understood, but they both thought Jesse was too young to have it.

Shelly continued her story. "After about a month, Bill said he was flying to Hawaii to find a job and send for us once he found a home. It was out of the blue, but I was young and didn't know any better."

"Dad was pretty skilled at hiding things and conning people." Liz was old enough to understand the things her dad had done to Shelly and to other people.

"Yes, he was. I'm surprised you remembered about some things he did."

"I remember a lot more than you realize," Liz added.

"Well, the days kept going by, and I never heard a word from him. Not even a letter to say how he was doing. One day I got a call from Thea up in Washington, and she said Bill was up there and not in Hawaii." Thea was related to Shelly, but not a blood relative.

"Thea told me he was living up there in Washington, near Tacoma. It seems he was living with the same woman he was cheating on me with when we lived up there. Bill had married her while still being married to me. Of course, their marriage was illegal and didn't count."

Brooke just sat there, holding her hand to her mouth in surprise and shaking her head. Liz had muttered a few choice words of condemnation.

"I was devastated and didn't know what to do. So the only thing I saw to do was to get out of Las Vegas as soon as possible."

"That must have been terrible. I understand how you feel," Brooke said.

Shelly knew a lot about what her sister endured with her first husband, so she nodded in acknowledgment.

"I didn't even pack up everything. Instead, I just took what I could fit in the car and drove with the kids to aunt Sherry and uncle Gil's in Northern California. If I remember right, I didn't even un-enroll you kids from school," Shelly said, looking over at Liz.

"I don't remember either," Liz replied. "We packed the things in the car and left rather abruptly."

"Once we got there, aunt Sherry and uncle Gil came outside. After giving us all a hug, uncle Gil looked at the car, especially one tire. He was shaking his head and saying he couldn't believe what he was seeing. Uncle Gil called me over to look at something. On the passenger side, the front tire had an enormous bulge in it, the size of a baseball or so. He said that the tire should have already blown out long ago, and that we were lucky to have made it there without wrecking."

Brooke nodded and commented, "I tell ya' Shelly, God was watching out for you and the kids. A blown tire on the highway could have led to disaster."

"That's what we all thought. We ended up staying with them for a little while. Uncle Gil drove to Vegas with his trailer and got the rest of our things. Thankfully, we found a little house to rent, and aunt Sherry helped me get the kids into the local school. I felt bad for you kids having to pick up and move to so many different schools."

"We had a lot of experiences, that's for sure," Liz added.

"Things were going okay, and aunt Sherry and uncle Gil were helping us with the rent. One day, I got a letter from Bill. It was a brief letter and he wrote that he had made a huge mistake and that he missed us. Bill also wrote that he was tired of Lily and her two kids and wanted to come back. Uncle Gil told Thea that we had moved back to California, so Bill found out where we were. I eventually took him back, seeing that our family would be better off with him making money, so we didn't have to rely on others."

"I can certainly understand why you took him back. Especially back in the older days," Brooke sympathized.

"I didn't find out until much later that Bill had moved Lily and her kids down to Vegas like he did with us. Bill abandoned them in Vegas the same as us," Shelly recalled.

"Do you think he told them he was going to Hawaii like he told us?" Liz wondered. She pitied Lily and her kids now that Bill had done the same thing to them.

"Who knows? In the middle of the school year, we picked up and moved back out to Indiana to be near Bill's mom and sister. That made for three different schools that you kids attended in the same school year."

"No. I'm pretty sure it was four," Liz corrected Shelly. "We went to two different schools in Vegas."

"I don't remember that. But there were lots of things I

had forgotten," Shelly added, a little frustrated at herself for not recalling events she should have remembered.

"Don't beat yourself up over that. Gary and I have that great long-term memory. Our short-term memory stinks, though." Shelly laughed along with the others. "I have trouble remembering what I had for lunch the day before. But ask me about something that happened thirty years ago, and I can tell you most every detail."

Shelly remembered a story her aunt Irene told her that had happened in California before the family moved back to Indiana. It was something that Bill may have done to Shelly. She might have blocked most of it out of her memory.

Shelly's aunt Irene and her family were living temporarily in California in the late 1960s for a little while. It was late in the morning, and Jesse, Liz, and Gary were at the local school.

Irene had received a call from Bill. "Irene, this is Bill. Something is wrong with Shelly. She's on the couch and not moving or responding."

Irene replied, "I will be right over." Thoughts started going through her head. She knew what Bill was capable of doing. She began to worry about Shelly.

After hanging up the phone, Irene, along with her sister, Sherry, got in the car and drove to Bill and Shelly's house. They only had to drive about three miles, but it seemed like a lot farther because of the circumstances.

Irene pulled the car into their small driveway, and she and Sherry walked up to the door. Instead of knocking on the door, they proceeded inside. Bill was standing at the opposite end of the living room, near the kitchen. Shelly was unresponsive on the couch on the other side of the room. Irene and Sherry noticed that there was a pillow covering part of Shelly's face.

"What happened here, Bill?" Irene demanded.

"She's not responding when I talk to her," Bill replied.

Irene became more suspicious and inquired further. "Bill, did you do anything to her?" Irene thought it was strange that Bill was standing on the other side of the room away from Shelly instead of at her side when she and Sherry first walked into the house.

"No. She was lying on the couch like that with the pillow over her face, and I tried to wake her. When she wouldn't come around, I called you."

Neither Irene nor Sherry seemed to buy his story. They both glared at Bill.

Irene spoke to her sister. "Sherry, help me get Shelly up and into the car. Bill! Sherry and I are taking Shelly to the hospital. You stay here and wait for the kids." Irene wanted to get Shelly away from Bill as soon as possible. Sherry and Irene each grabbed an arm, put it around their shoulder, and carried Shelly out to the car. Bill didn't even bother to help carry his own wife or open the door for her.

Once they got Shelly into the car and started driving to the hospital, she came around a bit. Shelly mumbled the words, "Don't let them lock me up." Irene knew what

Shelly meant by that. She had been all too aware of what Bill was doing to her.

Irene didn't end up driving to the hospital after all. Shelly seemed to recover and feel better. Instead of taking Shelly back to the house with Bill, Irene drove her over to Sherry and Gil's home. Once the kids got out of school, Irene picked them up with Shelly and took them back to Sherry and Gil's place. Shelly and the kids stayed there for a few days before returning home.

Irene and Sherry felt so bad for her. They knew Bill had, at times, tried to drive her to madness, so she might try to kill herself or have her committed. Shelly didn't leave Bill after this incident. They continued to live in California for a few more months before moving to Indiana.

"Mom, it sounds like Dad was trying to smother you on the couch with a pillow. After you went unconscious, he must have snapped out of his rage and then called Irene." Liz said.

"You're probably right, but to tell you the truth, I don't remember that. I don't remember any of that at all." Shelly replied.

Brooke sat on the sofa, stunned by what she heard. She shook her head in both disgust and anger at Bill and sympathy for Shelly.

Shelly continued the story. "A few months after the couch incident, we packed up the old Galaxy 500, rented a small moving trailer, and drove out to Indiana. We took Interstate 80 most of the way there."

"Didn't we stop at a few motels with swimming pools outside? Once we ate our dinner, us kids were in the pool immediately after," Liz reminisced about those good times in the motel pools. Back then, the pools were almost always outside and had diving boards.

"I had to clean up after you kids. Those swimsuits didn't dry quick," Shelly added.

Liz added, "We stopped at the Salt Flats, where they raced the cars for speed, and visited the Salt Lake itself. There were some other places we stopped at along the way, but I forgot some of them."

Shelly continued her story. "Well, once we got to Indiana, we stayed with Bill's sister and brother-in-law, Beth and Gene. The basement they had was nice and cozy. It had a full kitchen and a living room, and they had put a couple of beds down there. Jesse slept downstairs in the other bed near the one Bill and I slept in. Liz slept upstairs with Karen, and Gary shared Lee's bedroom. Lee and Gary were around the same age, and Liz and Karen were also about the same age. It worked out great."

"That must have helped the kids, having cousins their own age," Brooke said.

"Yes, it did. Jesse was a little older than Liz and Karen, but only by a year or so. That made things a little easier on him. Not long after we got there and settled in, Bill was able to get some work building a few garages and shops. It helped to get us some money. Enough that we could move out to a farm about a mile and a half outside the town. Bill started getting more work in the area building houses."

"Mom, I remember Jesse used to go with dad to help at the construction sites. Since he was about thirteen years old, there was a fair amount he could do other than using the power tools. He said he carried lumber and did some hammer and nail work. I think he did clean-up work as well. He spoke fondly of that time. Jesse told me that one of his favorite things about that was sitting next to dad with his lunch box and eating with sawdust all over him."

"I don't remember that too well. I know that Gary told me about the time he stayed back and helping your dad work on building a house when he was about eight. It was when Beth and Gene took us all to the lake to go water skiing in their boat," Shelly said.

Liz replied. "We had a lot of fun."

"I only recall a bit of," Shelly said. "Well, a little while later, Bill got a job at the RV factory nearby, where they built the motorhomes. The home building was not secure, and money was not coming in too much. I was glad to have a steady income," Shelly said.

Bill could not get that much work building homes and doing home repairs. There wasn't enough money from what he could do to make ends meet. Shelly had started a garden behind the house they rented. Shelly, Bill, and the kids lived on a farm that had cows by a barn and fields that would have corn and soy beans grown on them. The owner of the farm did all the work having to do with the farm. According to the rental agreement, Bill and Shelly had to maintain the house and mow the lawn.

"So many memories at the old farmhouse," Liz recalled. "The first one was the horrible smell from the cows. It stunk. After a while, we got used to it, and it didn't really bother us."

"I don't think I ever got used to it," Shelly said, shaking her head at the thought.

Brooke had been sitting quietly, listening to the story, but then asked Shelly a question. "Shelly, I'm curious about something. When did the trouble really begin that led you to want a divorce from Bill?" Brooke said. She had heard some things about what happened, but they were in bits and pieces. She was about to get the entire story.

"There were several times I wanted to divorce him, but the final straw was in early 1972, around March. One night when Bill and I were driving back from someplace in Fort Wayne. I was wearing a coat because it was cold outside. Bill turned the car onto a smaller country road to go home like we normally do. We had to stop at that train crossing because a train was going by. Bill looked over at me and said he could kill us both right there. Then he started to ease the car forward towards the train. It scared the heck out of me."

Brooke gasped at the thought. "I can't imagine how horrified you must have been."

"I was yelling at him to stop, but he kept saying he

would drive us right into the train and end it. He kept edging closer to it with the car. I opened the door to get out, and he grabbed my coat sleeve to stop me," Shelly said.

Liz interrupted while shaking her head, "What a jerk."

"Your dad did a lot of bad things to us," Shelly replied and nodding to Liz's comment. "I managed to slip out of my coat and run back toward the highway and cross it to a house on the other side of the road. I saw the lights on, and thank God the people were there. The couple at the door were in their mid to late forties. I was just thirty-two. If they hadn't been home, I don't know what might have happened or what Bill would have done. I turned back to see that he had driven off."

"God was watching out for you that night," Brooke exclaimed with a relieved look.

"He must have been, because I don't know if I looked to see if any cars were coming when I crossed the road," Shelly replied.

Shelly told Liz and Brooke about how she was frantic at the people's door and that they knew something terrible was wrong. The couple ushered her into the safety of their house. The woman brought Shelly into the living room and got her something to drink while her husband called the police to have someone come out. Shelly had never learned their names during all of this. The older couple must have understood that learning names wasn't a top priority.

"I told the man what happened so he could relay it

to the police. A little while later, a sheriff's deputy came out to take a statement and to bring me into the station. I thanked the people for helping me and then left with the deputy. When I got to the station, they filled out a restraining order against Bill and took me back home. Liz, I'm not sure if you remember this, but they made your dad pack some things and took him to your grandma's because of the restraining order."

"I remember some of it. I knew it was late at night, and I was tired," Liz said.

Brooke interjected. "Shelly! I'm curious about something. While this was going on, did you think he might go back to the house and try to do something to the kids, like take them away?"

Shelly thought about it for a moment. "I'm not sure if I did or not. I was so scared and angry at the same time it might not have crossed my mind."

Brooke shook her head in agreement and understanding.

Shelly continued to tell Brooke and Liz about the incident at the train crossing, what happened next. She couldn't take any more of Bill's abuses, so she separated from Bill and filed for divorce.

The following months after that night at the railroad crossing, Bill lived with his mom. The kids could visit Bill at his mom's, but because of the restraining order, either Bill's mom or his sister, Beth, had to be present during the visits.

Shelly told the rest of the story. The restraining order did little to stop Bill from stalking Shelly.

"I wished the troubles had stopped after the train incident, but they didn't. I was working in the town about seven miles away at a discount store with Bill's sister, Beth. One day, when I was coming home from work on the back country road I normally drove on, I could see Bill's car coming toward me. He steered into my lane and got this big smile on his face. Believe me! It wasn't a pleasant smile, either. I tried to steer into the other lane to avoid him, and he drove back over into my lane again."

Brooke gasped. What Shelly had told her horrified her. "How did you avoid him?"

"I moved back over to the right lane just before he got to me, and he drove right on by, staring at me with that terrible smile. I don't think I will ever get that look out of my head."

Brooke shivered and said, "I don't think I would have either."

"After that incident, he started stalking me at the discount store while I was at work. Bill would walk by the front of the store and look in as he walked past. He would also stand on the other side of the street and stare inside. Bill would just stand there and stare into the store and not move for several minutes. The older lady I worked with, Freida, would tell me to get in the back-room whenever we saw him outside. Thank goodness she knew what was going on."

"Freida was so nice to us. Jesse and Gary think so, too. She taught us some Christmas songs in German and how to say our ABCs and count in German as well." Liz reminisced.

"Freida was always nice to me," Shelly replied.

Bill's stalking of Shelly continued until about two or three days before Easter Sunday. What happened next would be the start of events that led to tragedy.

CHAPTER

14

EASTER WEEKEND

Liz would soon go back to Gary's house soon. He's going to drive Liz to the airport for her flight home to California. They made great strides helping Shelly deal with all the problems she had in her past that contributed to her depression.

Shelly has spoken with Liz and Gary in the past about the many conflicts with Bill. However, she did not have Brooke there to help her with the program that her sister had been getting help with.

Dinner time had come. Brooke, with Liz's help, fixed a delicious lasagna dinner with garlic bread and salad. The women needed an emotional break.

Once ready, the women gathered around the table and started eating.

"How's the lasagna?" Brooke asked.

"Delicious. I love it!"

"I agree. It tastes so good," Liz added.

Appreciative of Liz joining her and Shelly, Brooke said, "Liz, I am so glad you came here. Your mom really needed you during all of this."

"Wouldn't have missed it," Liz said. "Could you pass me some more salad?"

"Sure," Brooke replied, passing Liz the salad bowl.

She dished out more of the greens and asked her mom if she wanted more. "More salad?" holding the bowl up in Shelly's direction.

"Yes, just a little." Shelly replied. She has never been a big eater, especially when she's at a restaurant or at a house as a guest.

After they finished dinner, both Shelly and Liz complimented Brooke on another fine meal. Liz walked into the kitchen to help Brooke with the dishes. Shelly asked to help, but Brooke and Liz refused her offer and told her to sit down and relax.

After finishing the dishes, Liz brought out a cup of coffee for Shelly. She remembered how her mom liked it, and she already added in some cream and sugar. Shelly never cared for a lot of sugar in her coffee, only about a half a spoonful.

A few minutes later, Brooke joined Shelly and Liz in the living room. This time, Jonah laid at the feet of Liz. This surprised all three women and laughed at the dog's action.

"Jonah likes me better," Liz boasted, looking at Brooke.

"You traitor," Brooke replied looking at Jonah with a fake angry face, but smiled afterward.

After the laughter died down, Liz prompted the conversation.

"Mom, you left off before telling us about the first big attack after the separation."

"I'll start, but I will need your help for the things I can't remember," Shelly said.

Liz nodded.

Easter weekend, 1972. Shelly and her thirteen-year-old daughter, Liz, worked outside hanging up laundry on the clothesline. A light breeze ruffling clothes already hung on the line. The temperature was in the low seventies, but not very humid. The usual weather for this time of year in northeast Indiana.

Fourteen-year-old Jesse and nine-year-old Gary stayed inside the house. Jesse listened to his favorite rock music while browsing over the latest car magazine. Gary laid on the bed reading a Hardy Boys book called The Jungle Pyramid.

As Shelly hung up a shirt and clipped it to the line, she noticed a car pulling into the small turnout in front of their house. She immediately recognized the car and the man inside. It was Bill.

What's he doing here? Bill's not supposed to be anywhere around me. Shelly said to herself. A chill surged through her body. Fear overwhelmed her. Did he drive there to kill her?

"You stay here," Shelly commanded.

"Okay." Liz realized something was wrong. She said nothing more.

Being cautious, Shelly began walking over to Bill and his car. As she walked towards him, she looked back at Liz to make sure she had not followed her. Shelly then looked over at the neighbor's house on the other side of the road, down about fifty yards, give or take. Mel Rich stood outside working on his Econoline van. Shelly knew Mel carried an old revolver on him, or at least he kept it close by. Knowing Mel was outside helped to reassure Shelly a bit. But she knew what Bill was capable of.

When Shelly got closer to Bill, he spoke to her. His smile, not being genuine, looked sinister. Shelly became even more cautious, being familiar with the look.

"Hi Shelly. I want you to ride to Beth's with me so we can talk about either divorcing or reconciling," Bill says.

"You aren't supposed to be near here or around me."

"I know. Beth will be there. Come on. Get in the car now, and we'll drive over there," Bill pleaded.

Shelly stood in place, nervous and scared. She started shaking from fear. Shelly did not trust Bill after all he had done to her. She took a tentative step backward and looked over at the neighbor's house again, seeing that Mel still stood outside. If Bill made a move on her, she would yell for help or run over there.

Bill followed her line of sight and found her looking over at Mel. "Don't even think about it. You'll be dead before you get across the road," Bill said.

The way he said it scared Shelly so much more than what he said. Cold and sinister-like. The look in his eyes, maniacal, trance-like.

She looked back at Liz over by the clothesline and gave her a little smile. Liz smiled back, thinking her mom just gave her a reassuring smile, as if everything was going to be okay. It was not.

Shelly noticed a car cruising down the country road not far away. It was coming close, and just before the car got to where she stood, she ran across the road in front of the approaching car as fast as possible. She ran toward the neighbor's house, shouting for Mel to help her. Shelly was not much of a runner, but she had run faster than ever before.

Mel started running toward Shelly. Bill saw him and got into his car. He started it and looked back to see if he could turn the car around and run her down before she made it over to the neighbor running toward her.

Shelly ran into Mel along the road in between the two houses. It was too late for Bill to turn around. He remembered that Mel often carried a pistol, so he did not want to chance it. Bill put the car in drive and sped out from the side of the road, throwing pebbles in his wake.

Liz ran to her mom after Bill left. "Mom, are you okay? I heard everything." She was levelheaded for a thirteen-year-old girl after what she had witnessed. She wanted to run over to help while it was going on, but thought better of it.

"I'm okay now. Go tell Jesse and Gary to pack a few

clothes. We're going to grandma Ruth's for a few days," Shelly says.

Ruth was Bill's former stepmother. She never really got along with Bill, but Shelly and the kids often spent time with her. Ruth lived in Fort Wayne, and the drive would not be too long.

"Liz, make sure not to scare them. Especially Gary. Just tell him I've decided that we are going to spend a few days with grandma Ruth. You can tell Jesse what happened, but tell him when you are away from Gary."

Liz nodded, turned, and started walking back to the house. Shelly turned back to her neighbor, Mel. "Thank God you were outside. There's no telling what Bill would have done had you not been out here."

"Glad I could help, but I didn't really do anything," Mel replied.

"Trust me," Shelly said. "Just being outside and visible helped more than you think." Feeling grateful and relieved, she believed that had Mel not been outside, she might very well be dead.

"Do you want me to keep an eye on your place while you are gone?" Mel asked.

"Just glance over now and then to make sure he isn't there. If he shows back up, call the police."

Mel nodded, and they said their goodbyes. Shelly walked back to the house to pack a few things and get the kids ready.

"Liz, are the boys about ready?"

"I think so," Liz answered. "I have a few things in a bag."

Liz looked like she had something on her mind. Shelly realized that. She waited a few moments, giving Liz the chance to say whatever was on her mind.

"Mom. Are we going to be okay?"

Shelly looked at her and gave a reassuring smile.

"Yes. We are. Now go get Jesse and Gary and tell them to get into the car. I'll be out soon."

Shelly packed a few clothes and the toothbrushes. Ruth would have soap and toothpaste already. She hurried up, not knowing if Bill would come back.

Once finished, Shelly rushed out to the car and put her bag in the trunk of the old brown Dodge Dart. Liz was sitting in the front passenger seat, while Gary and Jesse were in the back. No one said much of anything.

Shelly started the car and pulled onto the road from the gravel driveway. She looked both ways to make sure no cars were approaching and that Bill was not around. As Shelly pulled out, she thought of getting to Ruth's as quickly as possible, but she didn't want to take the usual route.

The car ride to Ruth's took about twenty-five minutes longer than usual. Shelly drove on roads she didn't take before, avoiding the normal routes. She kept looking around and in her rearview mirror to see if she could see Bill's car. There was no sign of him. Shelly circled around the block where Ruth's apartment building was. Once she was convinced that Bill wasn't around, she drove into the parking lot and found a spot that was out of view from the street.

Shelly and the kids took their bags with them and headed to the elevator in the lobby. Once they got to the apartment door, Shelly knocked. Ruth opened the door and saw Shelly and the kids with their bags standing out in the hallway.

Ruth was aware of Shelly's troubles with Bill and didn't question why they were there. She just welcomed them. "Come in. Come in." Ruth said, smiling.

"Hi grandma," Gary said.

Jesse and Liz followed up with a greeting.

"Well, isn't this a wonderful surprise? Hello kids. Come on in," Ruth said, keeping a smile on her face. She could see that something was wrong.

Ruth looked at Shelly as she walked through the door after the kids. She did not have to ask how Shelly was doing. She could see the worry on her face. As Shelly walked by her and into the apartment, Ruth placed a comforting hand on her shoulder. Shelly almost broke down crying, but she held it together for the kids.

Shelly and the kids stayed at Ruth's little two bed-room apartment for two days, and during that time, the kids had fun visiting with their step grandma. When the three young ones went to bed, Shelly talked with Ruth about what had happened. Ruth knew Bill's problems. It didn't surprise her, but she was concerned for Shelly and the kids.

The two days at Ruth's went by fast, but they helped

Shelly calm down. She felt it was time to go home and that Bill would have calmed down enough. Besides, he would most likely be at his mom's place.

Ruth asked if they could stay a little longer since it was Easter Sunday, but Shelly had the baskets and eggs already made at home. It was their family tradition. She would hide eggs outside for the kids to look for. Now that Jesse and Liz were teens, they did this more for Gary.

They all said goodbye to Ruth after their breakfast. They got back into the car to head home. Shelly was eager to go home. She drove the fastest route she knew.

Shelly was worried that she might spot Bill's car at the house. She was ready to drive away if she saw his car parked there. She was relieved when it was nowhere in sight. That was a slight comfort to her. Shelly parked the car and told the kids to grab their things and head inside.

"Mom, there's something in the door."

THE FIRST ATTACK

Liz and Shelly continued telling Brooke the detailed story.

"Mom, there's something in the door. Looks like an envelope," Liz said, wondering what it could be. She started to reach for it.

This worried Shelly. "No, don't touch it. Liz, stay back behind me."

Liz got behind Shelly a few feet, looking at the piece of paper in the door. Jesse kept Gary out in the yard, playing with him to keep him away.

Shelly checked the door and wedged in it was an envelope. It was addressed to her and the kids.

She felt something a little bulkier in the envelope than just a letter. Shelly carefully opened it, not sure what she was going to find. When she opened the envelope flap, she pulled out the one-page letter folded in half. At the bottom of the envelope was a ring. Shelly pulled it out and realized it was Bill's wedding band. Shelly then opened the letter to read it. She noticed the writing was short.

Shelly,

Here is my wedding ring.

Sorry I put you and the kids through this trouble.

I hope you can forgive me.

By the time you find this letter, I'll already be dead.

I can't go on.

Love, Bill

Shelly covered her mouth with her hand and gasped. Was this for attention? Was he really dead? Shelly motioned for Liz to look at the letter. She made sure Gary didn't see it. Jesse was playing catch with him in the yard with the football.

Liz read it and looked at her mom. "Let's all get inside and call aunt Beth."

Shelly kept the kids in the kitchen downstairs. Liz made the phone call and told Bill's sister what they found. Beth said she would send her husband, Gene, over.

"Liz, would you go upstairs in the closet and get the Easter baskets? We can put them together and have a little Easter egg hunt. Gary would like that." Shelly wanted to help keep their minds off Bill and what was happening. Trying to have the Easter egg hunt and the dinner would help calm things down.

"Okay, mom," Liz said, then turned and walked upstairs. Not long after getting the baskets, uncle Gene was pulling into the driveway.

Shelly and the kids went outside to greet him. Gene brought his son, Lee, with him. Lee was a grade ahead of Gary, and they were best friends.

They walked up to the porch and Shelly met Gene at the door. "Let's talk inside. How about you boys go outside and throw the football around," Gene said to his son, Lee, and to Gary.

They moved inside the house, and Shelly showed him the letter and the ring. Gene read it while standing by the sink, leaning against the counter. He rubbed his mouth, contemplating what he just read.

"I don't know what to think, Shelly. Neither Beth nor I have seen him or his car for at least two or three days. I just can't imagine him doing this," Gene said.

"I don't really know what to think, either," Shelly replied. "What should I do?"

"Just stay here and keep the phone open. Let me go back and talk to Beth. See what she knows. For now, keep an eye out. If he comes by, don't let him in the house. Call me and the police."

"Thanks, Gene," Shelly replied, relieved that Gene was there and that he and Beth lived close.

Gene walked outside and told Lee they were leaving. Lee and Gary said goodbye to each other and said that they would play later. Shelly and the two younger kids walked back into the house. Jesse had stayed in the living room, watching TV, while Gene was there.

"Jesse! Come into the kitchen, okay? I want to talk to all of you," Shelly said.

"Okay." Jesse walked over to the television and switched it off, then joined Shelly and the other two kids.

Once Jesse was in the kitchen, Shelly started talking to the kids about a plan for what to do if their dad showed up. Gary stood in the open doorway between the kitchen and the living room, leaning against the door jamb, listening to the conversation.

A noise coming from the stairs on the far side of the living room that led to the upstairs bedrooms caught Gary's attention. There were footsteps coming down the lower part of the stairs.

Gary stared at the doorway to the stairs until he caught sight of his dad walking around the corner. Bill walked into the living room wearing his dark blue t-shirt with red sleeves.

"Mom, dad's here," Gary said, surprised that his dad was in the house. He wondered how he got upstairs. They had been home from Ruth's house for a while now.

"Gary, get into the kitchen. Get behind me," Shelly said firmly.

"What are you doing here?" She demanded, grabbing the letter and holding it up. "What was this about?"

"I didn't come here to fight," Bill said.

"Bill, you're not supposed to be here. Leave now," Shelly commanded.

"I want to talk," Bill replied. He was still talking in a calm voice. Calm but not peaceful. Bill had a sinister tone that made his calm voice frightening.

"I said get out," Shelly said, getting louder. "Get out now!" she shouted, now in near hysterics.

"Don't raise your voice at me. We need to talk," Bill commanded in a more demanding and fierce tone than before.

Shelly was losing it. She was screaming at the top of her lungs for Bill to get out and leave them alone. She was shaking and almost in tears. Bill started yelling. The situation was getting out of control.

"Gary, get out of the house now," Liz demanded. She was worried about Gary's safety.

Gary didn't question her. He ran out of the house through the side door. Jesse had already run out moments earlier. Despite being the oldest among the kids, the fighting hit him the hardest. Maybe it was because he was the oldest and had been at the receiving end of more of Bill's anger and hostility than either Liz or Gary. Liz hurried to the phone and called her uncle Gene, telling him that dad was there, that they were fighting, and to hurry and get over there.

Bill grabbed Shelly by the shoulders and shook her. Liz was shouting at him. "Dad, stop it! You're hurting her!"

Shelly yelled for him to get away from her. She was

in tears and shaking. She was losing control of herself and wanted to get away from him. Something suddenly made Bill stop what he was doing, and he took a step back. He looked over at Liz, and his expression seemed to change. He appeared a little calmer and more relaxed. Bill looked back from Liz to Shelly, then turned and walked to the door.

Jesse had run across the farm field to the small patch of woods a couple hundred yards behind the house. Gary ran out and was in the middle of the field when there was a noise behind him.

Standing in the middle of the field, not knowing what to do, listening to Jesse crying in the woods further out, Gary recognized a sound behind him near the house. He looked back toward the sound and saw his dad walking toward him near the garden in the yard behind the house. Bill stopped walking and seemed to sway back and forth. The next moment, he collapsed face-first in the yard next to the edge of the garden.

Back inside the house, Liz was trying to calm her mother. She did not have any luck. Shelly cried at a near screaming level. Liz's heart broke for her.

Liz heard her uncle Gene's car pull up in the gravel section in front of the house. She was relieved to know help was there. Liz had to handle so many situations at her young age, but this was beyond her. She looked over to see Shelly pulling out the kitchen drawers, trying to find the knives to protect herself. One drawer fell to the floor.

"Mom, stop it. Don't!" Liz pleaded. She was afraid her mom might hurt herself.

Gene and his brother-in-law, Jim, ran inside the house.

"Uncle Gene, mom won't calm down. Help her!" Liz pleaded.

Shelly was crying uncontrollably. She gripped a kitchen knife in her hand and frantically stabbed it in the air. It traumatized her beyond reason. Gene moved Liz out of the way and to safety. Both Jim and Gene cautiously moved in to get the knife away from her.

They grabbed Shelly's arm and got the knife away from her without getting cut themselves. While this was going on, Liz called the police and told them what was happening, asking them to hurry.

Outside, Jesse was still near the woods across the farm field behind the house. Gary started walking back to the house from the middle of the field.

He kept looking at his dad lying next to the garden. Bill didn't move. He continued walking closer to the yard. As he approached his dad, he saw he still wasn't moving. *Is he dead? Is he breathing*? Thoughts raced through his head. *Why is dad lying in the grass?*

"Dad? Dad! Are you okay?" He said while still standing away from Bill and not getting any closer.

When Bill never answered or moved, Gary turned to walk up to the house. He wanted to see if his mom and sister were alright. As he walked inside, he heard his mom shouting and crying. It was coming from the living room. He crept to the doorway, not sure what he would see, and found his mom lying on her side on the couch. His uncle Gene was on top of her, trying to calm her down and stop her from hurting herself. She was crying, and even though she did not have the knife in her hand, she was still making the stabbing motion. Gary had no reaction to this. He just stared. Maybe the shock of seeing his mom like this was too much.

Liz had told much of this story since there was a fair amount that Shelly's mind had blocked out. The trauma was deep in her. Too deep to remember a lot of what had happened.

"Shelly, I can't imagine what you went through and what that must have been like," Brooke said while crying, barely able to get the words out. "It must have been frightening to have gone through that."

Neither Shelly nor Liz were crying about this. They had discussed all of it in the past, at great length and frequently. Brooke knew about some generalities of what happened, but she never learned the details about what really happened on that day.

"Once the police came, they called for an ambulance to come and get dad," Liz said. "Once we told them about dad coming from the bedrooms on the second story, the police walked up there to investigate. They discovered dad had waited in the attic. The police said he must have been up there waiting for at least two days. They found his shoes and overcoat pushed back in the closet, hidden by other clothes. He could have been peering down at me when I was getting the Easter baskets from that closet."

Shelly and Brooke shook at the thought that Bill could have been peering down at Liz from the attic above.

The ambulance, along with the police, took Bill to the hospital. He had collapsed in the yard from dehydration and a lack of food from waiting up in the attic for as long as he did. Once Bill was stable, the hospital transferred him to the psychiatric ward in the same hospital in Fort Wayne, Indiana.

"Mom, there's something I never told you when aunt Beth and uncle Gene took Jesse, Gary, and I to visit dad in the psych ward. It was something I took with me, a last-minute idea. I told Gary about it just recently, but I never thought about it after that. I took a tube of lipstick in case dad tried to kidnap us or something like that."

Surprised by this new revelation, Brooke asked, "How could he take you if he was in the hospital?"

"When we got there, the staff escorted us to the psych ward and met dad in the hallway outside the rooms. One thing that stood out about that hallway was a young woman dancing around, swinging her arms around like she was alone in some meadow," Liz said.

"I think I can picture that," Brooke remarked.

Liz continued telling them how the doctor gave Bill the okay to visit the kids outside, in the hospital park, without supervision.

She continued, "Even though I was only thirteen, I thought it was weird that dad could see us outside with no one watching us. I was glad I brought that lipstick tube. I had it in my mind that if he tried to kidnap us, I was going to write a message on a bathroom mirror. Fortunately, that never happened."

Shelly shook her head. "Now, that makes me mad that the doctor would have allowed that, especially after what happened."

"When dad got out of the hospital, he stayed with Grandma. Things had been pretty good for several weeks. He didn't come around or even call. He may have driven by the house, but I never saw him."

"Not that much had happened afterward. Things seemed peaceful for a little while," Shelly replied. "However, I'm still a little upset at that doctor for letting your dad be alone with you kids."

Liz changed the subject a bit. "I need a bathroom break. We also need to unwind. Especially before the big story."

Both Brooke and Shelly agreed. They all took about a twenty-minute break to use the bathroom and get some snacks and something to drink. Once they sat down back in the living room, Shelly and Liz would talk about the big attack.

THE LAST ATTACK

Liz's stay at Aunt Brooke's house was nearing its end. There was one more story to tell. Both Liz and her mom would have to tell it; same with the first big attack after Shelly and Bill's separation. Shelly remembered little of what happened. Liz will have to help her with the story.

"I remember going with mom to get the pistol, but she had to fill out paperwork and do a background check," Liz said. "Mom could not get the gun that day, so she had to go back another day. Mom! Didn't Gary go with you to pick it up?"

"Yes, he did. Gary did not know why I was getting it. When we were there, he asked why I was buying the gun. I told him it was for target practice. That seemed to work for him. I was doing what the lawyer suggested. Since he was familiar with the attacks, he told me I might want to get a pistol, just in case. Gary didn't say anything more about it," Shelly said.

Things had been quiet since Bill's release from the hospital in Fort Wayne. In fact, they have been a little too quiet. Bill had not even stalked her at work, and it bothered her even more.

Shelly knew in her gut Bill wouldn't stay away for long. He was getting to a point where he could very well kill her and maybe even the kids.

"When I got the gun, I put it in my purse. I made sure to keep it with me. Even while I was at home," Shelly continued.

Late afternoon! May 1972. The weather outside was overcast, and it had been raining all day. The kids were home from school, and Shelly, Jesse, and Gary were in the kitchen, talking about their day. Liz was outside on the porch, sitting in a folding lawn chair, watching the rain come down. She noticed movement to the side of her at the other end of the open porch. Liz saw her dad walk up the steps to the porch on the side of the house. Once Bill got up the steps, he noticed all his things boxed up and sitting at the end of the porch. It angered him. "What's my stuff doing out here like a pile of garbage?"

Liz just shrugged, got up from the chair, and started walking inside to warn Shelly. Bill followed her to the door.

In the middle of the conversation between Shelly and the two boys, while in the kitchen, they heard the side door open and saw Liz come in. Before she could say anything, another person followed behind her.

There was Bill standing in the entrance, wearing a beige overcoat for the rain and his blue t-shirt with red sleeves.

Immediately, Shelly's voice was harsh with hatred and fear, "You're not supposed to be here."

"Let's talk, ok?" Bill said, like he was having a normal conversation.

"No. Get out."

The argument escalated and spiraled out of control. Liz had to do something to try to stop this.

She spotted Jim Iverson, the owner of the farm, driving out from the cow pen area to leave. Next to the kitchen window was a large ceramic rooster cookie jar. Liz grabbed it and threw it through the thin windowpane to get his attention.

The glass and soon after, the cookie jar shattered, but because of the rain, Jim never heard it. Liz started yelling for help, but he was too far down the lane.

Bill looked at the broken window and smirked. The last person who could help them was long gone.

"Gary, run out the front door. Now!" Liz shouted.

Gary didn't need to be told twice. He had never experienced something so frightening. Though the distance between the kitchen and front door wasn't far, it appeared distant to him. Nonetheless, he took off. Bill stepped over to block his way.

Gary looked up to discover his dad towering over him.

Bill's icy glare sent chills down his spine. "You're not going anywhere," Bill said.

Gary stopped dead in his tracks and backed up. He glanced to his left and saw Liz and Jesse running up to their dad and pushing into him like football players blocking on the line. "Gary! Get out behind us. Run. Run!" Liz and Jesse both shouted for Gary to leave.

When Gary ran out of the house, he didn't know what to do. It was raining out, and he stood in the grass, looking around. Gary saw the old car parked next to the garage, so he ran as fast as he could and got into the driver's seat, quickly locking all the doors.

Meanwhile, inside, the arguing was still going on. "Why in the hell is my stuff on the damn porch, huh? Bill shouted. He felt that since he paid the rent on the house, Shelly had disrespected him by putting his clothes and other things on the porch as if they were garbage.

Jesse couldn't take it anymore. He ran towards the woods, the same area he fled to during the first major attack. Ignoring the rain clinging to his clothes, Jesse felt sick with dread. Something bad was going to happen this time, and he knew it. Jesse wanted to run back to the house, after glancing back, and help his mom and Liz, but Jesse froze in place. He felt a touch of relief knowing that Gary hid in the car.

Bill pushed Shelly, yelling at her with blind rage. He hit her with an open hand, and his words bordered on incoherence. Liz grabbed his arm to pull him away, which did little to deter him from his rage.

With his keys gripped in his right hand, he swung them, aiming for Shelly's head. She raised up her arm to block the keys, which had dug deep between her thumb and forefinger.

Blood spurted out onto the floor. "Dad, for the love of God, stop it! She's hurt!" Liz shouted. She continued pushing him away, yelling at him to stop.

Bill never acknowledged her. His focus was only on her mom and nothing else. Shelly had her small purse with her and was reaching for her pistol. Her left hand still bled, and her heart pounded wildly, but she showed no sign of pain.

Knowing what her mom was reaching for, Liz moved out from between them, running for the phone. She held her breath with anticipation.

Shelly pulled the pistol out of her purse. A thin yellow scarf was covering part of the barrel and her hand as she lifted it from her purse.

Bill caught sight of the gun and stepped back. For a moment, he looked surprised. A few tense seconds passed before his face spread into a smile. He glanced at the pistol in Shelly's hands. Her gaze fixed on the gun as she trembled. Bill was within arm's reach.

The first bullet left the barrel. It hit Bill in the midsection. He bounced back. After a tense pause, his mouth spread into a grin as he moved toward Shelly. She pulled the trigger, again and then again.

Liz saw it all unfold and had a gut feeling her father was about to die. She watched as her mom desperately fired the pistol, staring at it in a stupor. Each time her dad got shot, he paused, then continued his advance.

Shelly shot Bill four times, three bullets in the torso and one in the left arm. With the last bullet, he stumbled back to the entrance by the main door. The rage that engulfed him faded as he fell to the floor. Propping himself up by his elbow, Bill weakly tilted his head toward Shelly and Liz. That demented smile was gone.

He fixed his gaze on Shelly. He stumbled with his words at first, then said, "I'm sorry for what I put you and the kids through," Bill struggled. His breathing becoming more ragged and unsteady. He let out a sigh and took one more breath before his last words. "Please forgive me."

The arm he used to support himself slid forward, and he died on his side, his arm extending from under his head. A pool of blood spreading larger onto the floor by his torso.

All the bullets spent. Five rounds came out of the revolver, and four of them hit Bill. The one round that didn't hit him shot into the living room and buried into a pillow on the floor.

The room was silent except for the clicking of the trigger. Shelly stared blankly at the gun, pulling the trigger to an emptied gun, until a set of gentle hands covered her own.

"Mom. It's over. Dad's gone. He's dead," Liz said in a reassuring voice. Throughout the ordeal, she didn't cry. Liz remained calm. Shelly stopped pulling the trigger and looked up at Liz afterward. She hadn't moved from the spot where Bill had attacked her.

"Is it over? Is it really over?" Shelly asked with mixed feelings.

"Yes mom. It's over." Liz replied.

The expected tears never came. The emotional weight that had culminated through every fight, every tense moment, had lifted. All sixteen years of it.

Once Liz made sure her mom would be alright, she moved over to the phone to dial the police. After explaining the situation, Liz called Beth and Gene to let them know what happened. Gene said he was coming over. After the phone calls, Liz took one more glance at Shelly to make sure she was okay, and then she headed outside through the other door to look for her brothers. Liz saw Jesse across the field, making his way back to the house. His hair had flattened to his head from the rain, and his eyes were heavy and bloodshot from the ordeal, but he was okay.

Liz then turned toward the car and jogged out to see if Gary was okay. The downpour had slowed to a drizzle.

Gary was sitting in the driver's seat of the car, so she went to the passenger side. He leaned over and unlocked the car door. Liz stepped in and looked over at Gary.

She was sure Jesse already knew. As loud as the rain was, he could hear the gunshots clear across the field. Gary was still so young. She took a breath, looked over, and said, "Gary, dad's dead."

Gary shook his head. He gave her a defiant look. "No, no, he's not."

"Yes, he is," Liz replied more firmly. "Mom had no other choice. She had to shoot him."

At that point, Gary jumped out of the car and ran up to the porch. He looked in the window of the door and saw his dad lying on the floor on his side with a large pool of blood next to him. His dad wasn't moving.

Gary had gone still and silent. His small figure stood like a stone at the door on the porch, transfixed by the sight of his father's body sprawled on the floor. "Gary? You okay?"

He never answered. He didn't move. Liz grabbed him by the shoulders and gently turned him around. He continued to stare at the ground.

Jesse made it up the porch when Liz asked, "Could you watch after Gary? I need to go inside and help mom."

Jesse nodded,"Dad's dead, isn't he? I had a bad feeling out in the field."

"Yes. Dad's dead."

Jesse numbingly took the news. He then took Gary by the shoulders and walked him back into the yard. The rain was letting up, and the sun was peeking out through the clouds.

Liz walked back into the house through the other door. She knew not to touch dad's body or move him. Shelly was sitting in the living room, holding a cloth to her hand, looking calm but numb. Liz started straightening up the inside of the house a bit. She didn't think about leaving it alone for the police to investigate.

Not long after, the police and the ambulance showed up and carried on with protocol. A deputy asked Liz to join her brothers outside. The weather cleared up, and the sun was glowing. She met Jesse and Gary at the well pump by the shed.

Gene had arrived at the house not long after the police. He went over to make sure the kids were okay, then talked to the police that were there. Since it was a small town, they all knew each other.

Jesse, Liz, and Gary watched as the paramedics rolled the stretcher up to the house. Inside, one paramedic put a bandage on Shelly's hand. She needed stitches. The keys that Bill hit her with tore her skin open and caused a deep wound. It had been worse since the keys were dull. She was lucky that it did not rip up any tendons or ligaments.

The paramedics had loaded Bill's body onto the stretcher and wheeled him to the ambulance. The kids watched as the paramedics led the stretcher through the grass. They saw the sheet covered over their father's head.

A few minutes later, the kids saw the sheriff escorting their mom out of the house. She wasn't in handcuffs. Since the prior attack, the local police station knew about the situation and could not blame her for what she did. The sheriff put a hand on Shelly's arm to console her.

Shelly looked at her kids. If anyone needed consoling, it was them. Knowing she couldn't go over to them just yet, Shelly held out her bandaged hand to say, See? I'm okay. She gave them a small smile and looked at their faces. They seemed to understand that it was over. Everything will be okay.

She turned her attention back to the sheriff. He waited until they were close to the squad car before he spoke to Shelly. "Mrs. Jorgensen, I am so sorry about what happened and for not being here to stop it. Ever since that first attack on Easter, I've had my deputies drive by here at regular intervals. I drove by here today about an hour before your daughter called. If only I had driven by again a little later. Please forgive me."

Shelly looked at him and said in a calm voice, "I don't blame you. You couldn't have known. I appreciate having the deputies drive by the house to check on us. It's all over now."

The sheriff escorted Shelly to his car and took her to the station for statements. Gene took the kids over to their house. When they walked into Beth and Gene's house, grandma Jorgensen was sitting in one of the dining room chairs and crying. Beth, standing next to her with her hands on grandma Jorgensen's shoulders, was crying as well.

SHELLY AND THE FUNERAL

The family gathered around grandma Jorgensen and Beth in the dining room. Once things settled down, Gene took Jesse out to his shop to work on a car to help take his mind off what happened. Liz walked to the bedroom with Karen to hang out and talk about what had transpired. Lee suggested that he and Gary play Nerf basketball in the garage.

The kids ended up staying at Beth and Gene's until the trial. They didn't have to wait long.

Shelly finished giving her statement to the police and had her hand stitched from Bill striking her with the keys. A sheriff's deputy then drove her back to her house. The first thing she did was call her father to tell him what happened. Jake told her he was getting on the first bus out there.

"Dad, you don't have to do that," Shelly said.

"I'm coming out there, and that is final. You said the kids are with their aunt and uncle. I don't want you to be there alone," Jake replied.

Shelly relented and admitted she wanted him out there. Jake said he would call her from the bus station when he got into town.

She spent the rest of the evening cleaning up the house, especially the blood stain in front of the door where Bill had died.

Bedtime came sooner than expected. Shelly was too tired to cry or do anything else that day. When the next morning came, she finished cleaning up what she could. The day was nice outside, and she didn't want to stay inside the house. Shelly took a lawn chair and sat outside by the large oak tree in the yard, trying to forget about the previous day's tragedy. Now and then, she would get up and walk around the yard, then stop and start to cry for a few moments.

Early in the evening the next day, the phone rang. Shelly answered it. Jake was on the other end. He was at the bus station in the nearby town, about five miles away.

"How did you get here so fast?" Shelly asked.

"Right after you called, I gathered up a few clothes and took a cab to the bus station, hoping they would have something. Sure enough, there was a bus leaving in about fifteen minutes. I managed to sleep through the night, and there were a lot fewer stops on this bus route. So, here I am." Jake said.

"Give me about ten minutes," Shelly said. Afterward, she started to smile and cry at the same time. Shelly was glad her dad was there. She didn't want to be alone. Shelly wanted her kids with her, but she also knew that Beth and Gene took good care of them for the time being.

The court hearing for the shooting was straightforward, taking place only about five days after the shooting occurred. Liz told the district attorney they were not to question Jesse or Gary. Neither of them were in the house when the shooting happened. She witnessed the entire thing, and she was to be the only one to testify.

Liz was just thirteen years old, and she handled the entire situation with great maturity. The testimony she gave about the shooting and the first attack helped bring a swift not-guilty by self-defense verdict. The time between the shooting and the verdict was just five days, which set a case precedent in the state.

On the day before the funeral, Shelly was trying to find clothes for the kids to wear to the service. She was having a tough time trying to take care of them, keeping her emotions in check, and tending to her drunk dad. Jake was not a mean drunk, but was always polite. Sort of cowboy gentleman like. The tragedies he faced with his son dying of cancer at an early age and his wife committing suicide drove him to drink. Shelly realized that, but it didn't make things any easier.

Not getting any help from her father, Shelly thought to call the preacher's wife, whose church they attended.

Shelly picked up the receiver and dialed the number on the old rotary phone. The phone rings a few times, and there is an answer on the other end. "Hello!"

"Hello. Mrs. Collins? This is Shelly Jorgensen."

"Oh! Hello," Mrs. Collins replied in a less than enthusiastic tone.

Shelly hadn't quite noticed the tone in her voice yet. "Could you help me out a bit. I'm trying to find the right clothes for my kids to wear to the funeral, but I don't know what to pick. I can't even find something for myself to wear. Can you help me out?"

"I don't know. I don't think I can help you. Goodbye!" Mrs. Collins said and hung up the phone.

Shelly couldn't believe that a preacher's wife could act this way. She stood in her kitchen, staring at the receiver for a few seconds, before snapping out of it and hanging up the phone. Shelly fought back a few tears. *How could she treat me like this? Doesn't she realize what Bill put me through?*

On the day of the funeral, the kids had been back at Shelly's for a couple of days now after their stay with Beth and Gene. Her father, Jake, had cleaned up and dress in crisp jeans, a cowboy shirt with a bolo for a tie along with clean cowboy boots and his cowboy hat. The kids were wearing darker clothes that Shelly put together. She had been so worried about the others that she only saved a little time for herself. The only thing she could find to wear at the last moment was a yellow dress.

Walking up to the funeral home after the quiet car ride from their home, Shelly could already see people gathering around the outside. Some people were walking inside the funeral parlor. Most people had dressed in dark suits and dark dresses. As Shelly and the rest walked up to the entrance, several people who were milling about looked over at her. Were they looking at her because of what she had done or because she was wearing a yellow dress to her late husband's funeral?

Shelly either ignored the stares or didn't even notice them. She continued to walk with her dad and the kids to the entrance. Reverend Collins stood at the bottom of the steps to greet her.

"Hello, Mrs. Jorgensen and kids," Reverend Collins said.

They all replied to him. "Reverend Collins! I'd like you to meet my father, Jake Gallagher," Shelly introduced each other.

Both Reverend Collins and Jake shook hands and gave polite greetings.

"Mrs. Jorgensen, you can go on inside to the room and spend a little time in there viewing Bill. There aren't many people in there yet. You should be able to see the row of chairs marked for you to sit on during the service."

"Thank you, Reverend," Shelly replied.

As they walked into the room where the service was to be, they saw the casket that Bill was lying in. Shelly told the kids to go see their dad while she stood back. All three kids walked up to the side of Bill's casket. None of them shed any tears. Gary was still too young to fully understand what was happening.

After the kids saw their father lying peacefully in the casket, grandma Jorgensen, Beth, Gene, and their two kids walked in the room. Karen and Lee walked over to Liz and Gary to be with them.

Grandma Jorgensen walked over to Shelly. She did something that surprised her. Grandma Jorgensen reached over and gently placed her hand on Shelly's hand. "I forgive you." she said.

At that moment, Shelly put her hand over grandma Jorgensen's and shed a couple of tears. Choked up, Shelly thanked her and tell her how sorry she was. Grandma Jorgensen gave a slight smile, then turned to walk back over to Beth and Gene.

More people were coming in, and everyone took their seats. Shelly could see several people who worked with Bill at the RV factory and people from their church. Gary's current third grade teacher, Gail Young, sat down in a chair next to Gary to help comfort him. Shelly was grateful and looked over at her from about four seats down to nod and show her gratitude.

The service was not too long. There was no mention of the fateful day of his death or what Shelly and the kids had gone through. Reverend Collins and some of Bill's friends and coworkers got up and spoke. Once the service was over, the casket and funeral procession drove about seven miles to the cemetery that would be Bill Jorgensen's resting place.

After the funeral at the cemetery, Beth invited Shelly and everyone to their house for some food and a get-together.

"Thank you, Beth. But I don't think I can keep it together. I can bring the kids over on the way home," Shelly replied.

"We have enough room to take them with us," Beth suggested.

Shelly and Jake drove home. After the get-together, Gene drove the kids back to the house. Shelly greeted them. She asked if they were hungry, but all three were full of the food that Beth laid out.

After a trying day, Shelly turned in for bed a little early. Jake and the kids stayed up for a while and visited. He told them some stories about his ranching days and when he was in the rodeo.

Gary had gotten tired and said good night to his grandpa and to Jesse and Liz. He walked up the stairs to his bedroom. Gary had to walk past Shelly's room first. He heard his mom crying. Not loudly, but a sort of weeping. Gary listened for a little while longer. He wondered if he should go in or not. In the end, he let his mother be.

Brooke had tears in her eyes. She had never heard the detailed story before.

Shelly continued to tell Brooke about their dad's state and staying drunk most of the time until he left. She said that she had to spend so much time making sure that Jake was okay.

Liz sat up straight. A look of realization flashed across her face.

"Mom, I just thought of something."

"What is it?" Shelly asked.

"Did you ever think that maybe God sent grandpa to you in that condition for a reason?"

"I'm not sure I follow."

"Well, we were staying at aunt Beth and uncle Gene's place, and you were at home with grandpa. Maybe God sent grandpa to you in that condition to give you something to focus on. He was able to get a bus that night, and it had a lot fewer stops than normal. You had to take care of him. He gave you a reason to stay busy and not think about what had just happened. Grandpa had somehow made it there in what seemed like record time, as you had said. What might have happened to you if grandpa had not been there and we had left you alone for too long in your condition?"

Brooke shook with a shudder. "Oh my goodness. That gives me chills just thinking about it. Shelly, I've always said that God works in mysterious ways, and after hearing what Liz said, I think he put dad there to keep you from possibly doing something horrible."

"I had never thought of it that way," Shelly said. She thought about the possibilities a little more. "When dad was there, I was mad at him because of his drinking and laziness. Little did I know he could have kept me from doing something to myself that could have affected you kids for the rest of your lives."

"Yep," Liz said, giving a warm smile. "Just remember that."

Shelly paused a moment to ponder it. She grabbed a tissue from her side table and wept, reflecting on how cruel life was for her kids. They never should have gone through that, especially with how young they were. If she had gotten away sooner.

"Look at what I put you kids through. You had to go through all of those moves to different places and the attacks from your dad. I just wouldn't know what to say to you kids to make it right." Shelly sniffled and wiped her nose.

Liz sat close to her and leaned over. She put her hand on Shelly's arm and said, "How about saying you're welcome?"

"What do you mean?" Shelly asked, blotting her eyes.

"I mean, you protected us kids. You protected us from dad. You made sure we had not just a house but a home. We always had food to eat. We always had a roof over our heads. Even the time when dad left us stranded in Vegas, you made it work."

Shelly and Brooke started to sob and weep at this revelation. Brooke spoke to her sister. She gestured with her hand and arm out to point to Liz.

"Shelly, do you need more proof that we love you?

Your kids adore you, and they know what you have done for them," Brooke wept into her tissue.

"Mom, I remember the doctor had looked at dad's psych records, and he was convinced that if you had not shot dad that day, he would have killed you. He could have killed us kids, as well. So I will say again. The only thing you can say to us about this is 'you're welcome'. Do you get what I mean?"

Shelly nodded her head while wiping her nose after crying. "I get it. I really do. But that was a long time ago. You all have your own families and just don't need me anymore."

Liz was still sitting close to Shelly. "Mom, we love you. Kevin and I drove a thousand miles out of the way to visit you when we took the RV to Florida for the race."

"Yes, but you only stayed with me for about a day and a half," Shelly said.

"Mom, we stayed three days. But remember, we had just finished a big trip from California to Florida. We were tired and wanted to get home. I asked Kevin if he was okay with driving up to Indiana or if he wanted to get home. He said he wanted to get home, but it was important to go visit you. If we didn't care about you, mom, would we have driven a big RV a thousand miles out of the way to see you?"

Shelly could finally see what her daughter, Liz, was talking about. She understood that her kids, now all grown up with their own kids, would always need her, but it's different from when they were little. She started smiling through the tears that were drying up. A light, a sort of sparkle, appeared in her eyes. Something in Shelly changed. Liz's words struck deep inside her. She tried to help her mom before, but they didn't have Brooke's help and experience.

"Look at you smiling now, mom. That's what I want to see," Liz said.

"I can't explain, but it's like an emotional weight being lifted from my body. A release of bad feelings," Shelly beamed. She had never experienced this. It took a few moments for Shelly to process her emotions.

Brooke noticed some of the change and could see an improvement in Shelly's attitude. Liz's words helped cut through her mom's depression. Brooke had been helping Shelly with the program that she used to help herself from her church. It was a step-by-step program that was supposed to take several weeks to reach the level that Shelly had reached in such a short time. Shelly still had a little way to go, but she has come far. There were a few more hurdles to face.

Liz got up out of her chair and leaned down to hug Shelly. Brooke smiled and wept, wiping the tears with a tissue. After Liz finished hugging her mom, both Shelly and Brooke stood up and hugged each other. Liz joined in, and all three embraced each other.

"Shelly, I am so proud of how fast you came through this. Your healing was much faster than I had made it through in my healing process. I think God saw just how bad of shape you were in and how close you were to just giving up. It was so miraculous," Brooke exclaimed.

"It really was," Liz added.

"And you, kiddo," Brooke said to Liz. "You have done wonders in helping your mom through this. She couldn't have gotten through this without you."

"We both were instrumental in this. I just hope she can continue this healing and not go back," Liz proclaimed.

Shelly said nothing while Brooke and Liz were talking; she just listened and nodded

The day was getting late. It had been an emotional rollercoaster for the three women. In the morning, Brooke was taking Liz and Shelly over to Gary's home for Liz's last night before her flight home, so this was to be an early night.

Brooke walked over and hugged Liz in a tight embrace. "I am so glad you could come. Your mom needed this more than you could know."

"I wouldn't have missed it, aunt Brooke."

Brooke let go and gave her niece's arm a squeeze before they said goodnight.

Next morning, after a light breakfast, they packed up the car. The trip was pleasant, with conversations about nothing in particular. Brooke dropped them off at Gary and Jessica's house. She came in to say hello before leaving for her appointment.

They spent the rest of the day chatting about various topics. Liz and her niece, Rylie, talked a lot about how she was doing and common girl things. Rylie was a little on the quiet side and would not talk much in a larger group, but Liz had her gabbing away a great deal. They looked through old pictures of the family, of old grandparents and great-grandparents.

Brooke stopped in for dinner later that evening. They gathered around the table to eat spaghetti and meatballs with salad and breadsticks. Brooke started the prayer.

"Dear Lord, thank you for this wonderful meal that Jessica worked hard at. Bless this wonderful family. Thank you for guiding Liz up here to help her mom. Bless my awesome sister and thank you for helping her get better. In Jesus' name, we pray, Amen."

Everyone else repeated, "Amen."

Liz's flight did not leave until the early afternoon. The morning of the flight, Jessica fixed a breakfast of homemade pancakes and link sausage.

Liz was grateful. "Jessica, you're spoiling me. These pancakes are wonderful. Where did you get this sausage? I've never tasted anything like it in California."

"Thank you." Jessica replied. "We get the sausage from the local grocery store. This brand comes from Montana. It's a little pricey, but worth it."

"It sure is." Liz agreed. Everyone else nodded in agreement as well.

The time had come to take Liz to the airport. She warmly embraced Jessica and Rylie. Jeff had already left for school, and Liz said her goodbyes to him before he left. Shelly rode with Gary to drop Liz off at the airport and then drive back to Brooke's. The sisters still had another four or five days of visiting before Shelly went to Gary and Jessica's home before boarding the train back to Indiana.

Liz said her goodbyes at the drop-off in front of the terminal. It had been a fulfilling trip for her, and she was happy she made the trip. Liz hadn't seen her mom look this content in ages. Perhaps ever.

"I love you, mom. You look like you're doing so much better," Liz said while holding her mom tightly.

"I love you, too. You've helped me out so much," Shelly said, giving Liz a loving pat on her back before letting go, watching her turn to Gary.

Liz went to hug him. "Come here, little bro'. You take good care of her while she is here. Thanks so much for getting me here and shuttling me around."

"My pleasure. Tell Kevin I said hi," Gary said.

Liz then grabbed her small suitcase with wheels and purse and headed into the terminal. Once in the door, she looked back and waved.

RENOUNCEMENT RENEWAL

After dropping Liz off at the airport, Gary and Shelly headed to Brooke's home. Shelly would spend another three or days there before going back over to Gary and Jessica's place before leaving on the train to go back home.

While driving away from the airport terminal, Gary commented on the change in his mom. Change that was for the better. "You are definitely looking much better and it shows in your face."

"I tell ya' Gary, I am doing so much better. Far better than when I first came in on the train," Shelly replied.

"What does Aunt Brooke have planned for you now?" Gary asked.

Shelly pondered the question for a moment. "There

are more things for us to go through on that program she has been going through from her church. The program is supposed to take several weeks, but Brooke has been speeding it up for me since I'm here for such a short time," Shelly answered.

"Looks like it's working," Gary commented. He has seen the change in his mom's face and in her eyes.

Shelly and her son, Gary, continued talking about her trip to Idaho and what was going on with her back at her home in Indiana. The forty-five-minute drive from the airport to Brooke's house was pleasant and went by fast.

Once they pulled into Brooke's driveway, Gary carried Shelly's small bag for her, and they walked up to the door. Instead of knocking, Shelly opened the door to her sister's home and walked in.

"Hello!" Shelly announced. "I'm back."

The first to greet them was Jonah, the Schnauzer, barking and running to them. Jonah barked at all the visitors, not in anger or fear, but to be petted. It was his way of greeting them. Jonah would not stop barking until the visitor or visitors gave him his required petting.

Gary bent down and petted the anxious and excited Jonah. He got down on the ground and rolled around a bit with Jonah. The two of them have that sort of relationship. Every now and then, Gary and Jessica watch Jonah for Brooke when she has to go away for a little while and can't take him with her.

Brooke walked up and greeted Shelly and Gary and asked, "Did you get Liz to the airport, okay?"

"Yes, we did," Shelly replied.

Gary spoke, "Well, I need to get going and leave you two to your visiting."

"Thanks so much for bringing Liz here, Gary. It meant so much to your mom and me. That was pretty sneaky the way you did it by tricking us, but that's going to make for a great story," Brooke said.

"I guess it will," Gary replied. "Bye, aunt Brooke. Bye, mom. See you in about three or four days days."

Both Shelly and Brooke said goodbye to Gary. He turned to leave, and as he was leaving, Gary petted Jonah one last time.

"Shelly, are you hungry?" Brooke asked after Gary left.

"Not really. I ate a good breakfast over at Gary and Jessica's. You know how good of a cook she is. When I was over there, she spoiled me. I didn't have to lift a finger. I could use some coffee, though," Shelly said.

Brooke poured her sister a cup of coffee, and she poured a cup for herself. While Brooke was getting the coffee, Shelly put her small bag back in her room and went to the bathroom. After finishing, she walked back out to the living room. Brooke sat on the sofa, Jonah lying next to her, without a care in the world.

"Got your coffee right next to your chair," Brooke said, pointing at the coffee.

"Thanks," Shelly replied. She reached over and grabbed the coffee cup.

"We are at a point where we can move forward in this program to the devotionals and renouncements. You've come so far in such a short time," Brooke said. "I'm really impressed."

"I couldn't have done it without your help. Or Liz and Gary's help," Shelly commented. "By the way, what do you mean by renouncements?"

"They're a series of statements to God and yourself that you renounce. A declaration to rid yourself of destructive emotions and negative thoughts," Brooke answered. "Once we begin reading, you'll get a better idea of what renouncements are."

Shelly nodded her head in agreement. She trusted her sister's plan to help her. It has been working out great so far.

For the next two days, Brooke shared different Bible passages with Shelly that she highlighted in the program she had been using. The writers of the program selected each verse to help with the problems people generally had. Brooke would explain each one to Shelly. Then they would talk about how each passage related to them.

Neither of the ladies shed any tears during these discussions. There had been a lot of crying during the talks about their past and the trials and tribulations each woman facedin their past. Brooke joked they should have bought stock in tissues.

Brooke had seen her sister make great strides since the train trip out to Idaho. She was not sure if Shelly's fully healed yet. There was one section in the latter part of the program that she needed to bring up with her sister.

"Shelly! There is something here I wanted to bring up with you. It's a little later in the program, but I think you're ready for it."

"I thought we had gone through most of it. I wonder what it is," Shelly replied.

"Well! There's a section that deals with being able to look at yourself in the mirror. If you have had a lot of emotional trauma in your life, then you'll most likely not be able to look at yourself in the mirror," Brooke said.

"I look in the mirror. I brush my hair in the mirror," Shelly commented.

Brooke could tell her sister did not quite get what she meant. She had to go into more detail and explain further.

"What I mean is that a person can't gaze into their own eyes. Instead, they find other things to focus on instead of their eyes. Even their own faces," Brooke explained.

Shelly just nodded, but Brooke discovered that this needed more work. She had another hurdle to get over. Brooke saw Shelly was making fast progress and she hoped her sister would get past this hurdle. She let it go and continued reading the Bible passages.

A little later in the day, Shelly walked into the bathroom and would try to stand in front of the mirror and look at herself. She tried, but all she did was glance everywhere else. Shelly looked at her hair, at her arms, and at the necklace she was wearing, but she still could not gaze into her own eyes. Throughout her life, Shelly could never look at herself in the mirror. She always thought she looked ugly. Shelly hated looking at her own face and believed it was too wide, too fat. There wasn't one nice thing she had ever said about her own appearance. Compliments from people about her appearance made her uncomfortable and she felt undeserving of the praise.

The next day was more of the same. Later in the evening, Brooke instructed Shelly on the renouncements. She told her to read them. Shelly began reading the renouncements to herself.

Brooke interrupted her. "Shelly, read them out loud. That way, it makes more of an impact."

Shelly started reading them out loud. There were two pages of them. After reading for a little while, the words started blending together, and she felt like she was going through the motions. She stopped after the first page.

"Brooke, I'm getting sleepy. I think I'll finish this tomorrow."

"Yeah, I am getting tired, too. Let's turn in. Tomorrow is your last full day here before you go back to Gary and Jessica's," Brooke said.

"Yep. The time has flown by fast." Shelly replied. "On one hand, it seems like I just got here. On the other hand, I've made a lot of progress from the talking and crying we've done. It seems like I've been here for a lot longer."

"I know what you mean," Brooke commented in agreement.

Shelly woke up early the next morning at five o'clock. She's been an early riser all her life. But the three-hour time difference between Indiana and Idaho made her wake up a little earlier during her visit.

She went out into the kitchen, where Jonah had greeted her. "Hi little buddy," she said to a happy Jonah, reaching down to pet him.

Shelly walked over to the counter to start the coffeemaker. Brooke had filled the water tank and added fresh grounds the night before, so all Shelly had to do was turn on the machine. It made the all-too-familiar gurgling sounds.

While the coffee was brewing, she started her morning bathroom routine, which was a ritual. Shelly put in her hearing aids; placed her dentures in her mouth; brushed her hair; and brushed her teeth.

Once she finished with that, the coffee was ready. She noticed Brooke was still be asleep. Her bedroom door was closed. Shelly took her coffee out to the living room, grabbed her devotionals and renouncements to read, and sat in the recliner in the living room.

After she finished reading her devotionals from page one again, Shelly started reading the renouncements on page two. The coffee in her cup was getting a little low, so she would get more coffee after she finished the second page. Shelly read them out loud, but in a quiet voice so as not to wake up Brooke. She was down to the last three.

I renounce the lie that I am rejected, unloved, or shameful.

In Christ, I am accepted.

I renounce the lie that I am guilty, unprotected, alone, or abandoned.

In Christ, I am secure.

I renounce the lie that I am worthless, inadequate, helpless, or hopeless.

In Christ, I am significant.

Shelly finished the last three renouncements, but didn't feel any different. She wondered if the renouncements were working for her.

With her empty coffee cup, Shelly got out of the recliner and walked into the kitchen to get a refill. As she walked back into the living room, something came over her. Shelly stopped walking and this sudden warmth poured all over her. She experienced an overwhelming powerful love for all of her family and friends. It seemed to come out of nowhere, appearing out of thin air. A huge smile came over her face.

I want to tell Brooke. Shelly thought. *I want to share with her what I just encountered. It is so amazing.*

She felt like she was on cloud nine and wanted to wake Brooke to tell her, but let her sleep instead. Shelly decided she would tell Brooke when she woke up.

Shelly shared with Brooke what had happened that morning after reading the renouncements and they agreed. The sudden feeling of internal warmth and love must have been a delayed reaction.

"Oh Shelly. I am so excited for you. Do you realize it takes most people several weeks or even months to get to this stage in the program? God had seen just how badly you needed help," Brooke said, starting to tear up.

Shelly started to tear up as well, while smiling. This time, the tears were not from their troubled and emotional past. They were tears of joy from Shelly's miraculous revelation.

"Shelly, I tell ya'. It's a miracle. I can see a change in your face and your eyes," Brooke proclaimed.

Brooke saw a change but knew her sister still could not look at herself in the mirror. She thought it was about to happen. Patience! One step at a time.

The rest of the day was easygoing. Shelly and Brooke read a few more renouncements. Afterward, they just talked about current events with the family and reflected on how far Shelly had come since she first arrived at Brooke's.

The next morning, they had a small breakfast. Shelly and Brooke were meeting with Shelly's daughter-in-law, Jessica, and Jessica's daughter, Rylie. They were going to have coffee at a nearby coffee shop. Shelly was then going to go home with them afterward to spend the rest of her trip there.

Brooke helped Shelly carry her small bag out to the car. Shelly had left her larger suitcase at Gary's house.

At the coffee shop, the four ladies sat around the table at the coffee shop, drinking coffee and eating the little pastries the shop served. They were all enjoying the ladies' day out.

Rylie was nineteen years old and living at home. She attended the local college and could save money by staying at Gary and Jessica's. Rylie worked at a nearby grocery store in the produce department.

The conversation remained light. Jessica could not help commenting on how great Shelly looked and that there was a light in her eyes that had not been there before.

"Mom, you look great. I can see just how much better you are. Your eyes are shining," Jessica said.

Shelly beamed with a big smile. In the past, a compliment would have made her uncomfortable. She would have tried to deflect it somehow. Shelly did not deflect it this time.

Seeing how much Shelly has changed, Jessica looked at Brooke. "You have been amazing with mom. You deserve so much credit for this. I also want you to know something. I am very proud of you. You experienced and endured so much trouble and hardship in your life. Some people would turn bitter and use that as an excuse to do bad things or be mean to others. But you are kind to everyone, and you're always very helpful to people, whether they are family, friends, or even strangers. Your hardships have strengthened you and are more beautiful all the way down to your soul."

Brooke was so touched that she started shedding a

few tears. Grabbing a napkin, she reached over and took Jessica's hand in her own hand.

"Jessica, what you just said touched me and moved me so much. I will never forget it. Thank you so much. Look at me. I'm shaking now," Brooke said. Jessica's thoughtful words moved her.

Shelly and Rylie both agreed. Shelly reached her arm around Brooke and squeezed her from the side.

The rest of their visit at the coffee shop centered more on Rylie and Jeff. Jeff was in high school and played football. Shelly told Brooke how neat it was to see her grandson play football and how good he was.

It was time to go back to Gary and Jessica's. The women said their goodbyes in the parking lot and moved Shelly's bag to Rylie's car.

"Oh, it was so good having you stay with me for so long. I don't think we have ever been able to spend time like that with each other," Brooke said.

"No. We never really did. We always had our husbands and kids around. I can't believe how much I never knew about you and what you endured," Shelly replied.

"We need to get together like this more often," Brooke said. "I'll stop over the day you leave. I know that Gary and Jessica are taking you to the Spokane train station late at night, so I'll drop by in the afternoon."

"Sounds good."

Shelly, Jessica, and Rylie got in the car to go to their house. The ride back was pleasant. Shelly enjoyed staying with her sister. But she was also glad to get back to Gary and Jessica's. She loved how Jessica spoiled her.

CHAPTER

19

THE MIRROR

The three of them returned home from having coffee with Brooke and bringing Shelly back to Gary and Jessica's house. Gary was at home, waiting for them to return. Jeff was still at school.

Shelly was glad when they pulled into the driveway. She had gone through a lot at Brooke's and had made great strides. Shelly was glad to relax now.

Gary greeted them at the door, and he immediately noticed a change in Shelly. "You look great. I can see the change in your eyes even more than after we took Liz to the airport." Gary commented.

"I am much better. You know how I was when I got here, right?

"All too well. You looked defeated and ready to give

up when you got here." Gary replied. The way Shelly looked and her words when he spoke to her on the phone before her trip caused him great concern. Liz had also voiced her concern to Gary. What he was seeing now from his mom was a whole different woman.

They spent the rest of the day talking to each other about current events and what her Rylie and Jeff have been doing. It was more of a relaxing day. Shelly had an emotional rollercoaster at her sister's place that helped lead to her healing. She needed a little break.

The next morning, Gary woke up and walked downstairs to his computer. The comfortable futon Shelly had been sleeping on was also in the same room as the computer. She was already awake and had gotten her a cup of coffee.

"Good morning, mom. How did you sleep?" Gary asked.

"Better than I have in a long time," Shelly replied.

Shelly began telling Gary about all she had done at Brooke's house.

"It all started with Brooke telling me about what she had gone through as a little girl and as a teen. Because of our age difference, we didn't spend much time together in the past, so there was a lot she told me I didn't know about."

"Can you tell me some of it? I know a little of what she went through with Adam." Gary replied. "But I never heard about her experiences as a kid."

Shelly told Gary about the hardships Brooke had experienced after their mom died from a self-inflicted gunshot wound. She told him about Brooke and their dad living in different places, where she spent most of the days alone and did not have friends to play with. Shelly told Gary about Brooke going out as a young girl looking for pop bottles to exchange for money.

The story of Brooke living with her aunt and uncle and being taken back to California by their dad. Then, being abandoned again back in Idaho showed Gary what Brooke had gone through.

"I never knew any of that about aunt Brooke," Gary said, surprised. "She never mentioned any of those things to me before."

"Brooke never said anything to me in the past, either," Shelly replied.

Shelly continued telling Gary about when Brooke and Adam's boys were little and they all lived in California. Then she told him about Brooke and Adam separating for a little while. That was, until Adam said he wanted to get back together with Brooke, what her reaction was, and how Adam replied to her.

Gary shook his head in disbelief and replied, "What a jerk."

"Did you know about Brooke and Adam and the boys living on a bus for a couple of years? Shelly asked.

"I heard a little something about it," Gary replied.

"She told me and Liz about this not long after the day you showed up with Liz and surprised me, you little stinker." Shelly kidded.

Gary laughed at his mom's comment and reflected

on that moment. "Your expression when Liz walked into the living room was priceless. Aunt Brooke's reaction on the top of the steps was also pretty awesome."

"I wasn't expecting her, and since I couldn't see Liz very well in the other room, I thought it was the neighbor lady. It took a few seconds for me to recognize who it was."

"I will never forget that," Gary said.

"While Liz was there we talked about my mom, about Brooke and then we talked about what I had gone through with your dad. We shed a lot of tears talking about our childhood and what Brooke and I suffered through with Bill and Adam."

"I bet there was a bunch of wadded-up tissue littered all over the floor," Gary said jokingly.

"Not that far off," Shelly replied.

"Once we dropped Liz off at the airport and you took me back to Brooke's, we read more of the program that she was walking me through. There was one part that was called renouncements. They were a bunch of sentences about renouncing many of the negative things surrounding my life."

Gary was on the edge of his office chair, listening to what his mom was telling him. He had seen the amazing transformation she has gone through.

Shelly continued, "The next morning, I woke up early and Brooke was still sleeping. I started reading the renouncements out loud but quietly since I didn't want to wake her up. When I finished, I got another cup of coffee. I didn't notice any difference after reading it, and I thought nothing of it. When I started walking back to my chair, I stopped and got this immediate sensation of overwhelming warmth and love."

"Did you wake up aunt Brooke to tell her?" Gary asked.

"No. I didn't want to wake her. But what I experienced was a sudden, overwhelming love for all my kids and all of my friends. It's hard to describe exactly what I felt, but right there, at that moment, I was sure I had achieved something great in my life. It was like I just crossed a very high emotional hurdle."

"That is so great, mom. It really shows." Gary was excited for his mom.

Shelly told him more about what Brooke and she had discussed. She told Gary about looking into the mirror.

"What do you mean about the mirror? What did it have to do with you?" Gary asked.

"Well, she told me that many people who experienced emotional trauma have trouble looking at themselves in the mirror. I mean, they cannot look into their own eyes. So a little later, after Brooke told me about it, I walked into the bathroom and tried looking into the mirror at myself. I was sure I was healed emotionally, but I guess at that point I still had some ways to go."

Gary sat, listening to his mom's story. He noticed where this was going and got an idea in his head. Shelly continued to tell the story.

"When I looked into the mirror, I still could not look directly into my eyes and just gazed elsewhere, like at my hair and my necklace. So after that, I just let it go and didn't try again."

Gary acted on the idea he just had while Shelly was telling him about the mirror. He sensed an opportunity to help get his mom past this hurdle. Shelly had come a long way so far with the help of Brooke and Liz. He had to do his part and get her past this hurdle of not being able to look at herself. This was her last hurdle.

"There's a saying that the eyes are the windows to the soul," Gary said.

"What do you mean?" Shelly asked, not understanding what Gary was saying.

"It means that whatever your emotions are inside your mind and heart, they show through your eyes," Gary explained. The opportunity had come for what he had to do next.

In the next moment, Gary got out of his chair, took a step toward Shelly, and extended his hand out toward her.

"Mom, come on. Come to the bathroom mirror with me." Gary said.

Shelly hesitated and shook her head. "No, that's okay. I'm fine." Shelly replied. Her expression showed she still had some anxiety about looking at herself. She did not want to face the mirror again. Shelly had come a long way, but she had not overcome this yet. perhaps she was afraid that by looking at herself in the mirror, she would regress to where she was before the trip.

Gary didn't accept that. He reached out farther, took his mom's hand, and gently pulled her up.

"Mom, we are going to the bathroom. It's time you face this." Gary commanded. He would not take no for an answer.

Shelly relented and followed Gary to the bathroom. Once inside, Gary positioned his mom in front of the mirror. There was no backing out for Shelly now. Gary would not let her. She had to face this.

"I want you to look into the mirror," Gary told his mom. "What do you see?"

Shelly looked into the mirror but still did not gaze into her eyes. She looked elsewhere. "I don't know," She replied.

Gary saw that she was looking everywhere except at her own eyes. He had to try something different. "Mom, turn toward me. Now, look into my eyes. What do you see?" Gary prompted.

Shelly was still a little confused or hesitant. Gary knew she was going to need more prompting. He thought he would try a different approach.

"Are they kind eyes? Are they warm?" Gary asked.

Shelly looked into her son's eyes, searching for what he had asked her.

"Well, yes. You do have kind eyes."

Gary saw this as a chance to get his mom past this big hurdle. It was going to happen. He could sense it. It was the last hurdle for his mom.

"Mom. My eyes are your eyes. I have your eyes. Do you understand? Gary said.

The expression on Shelly's face was that of understanding. Gary noticed the opening. His mom was ready for this. He jumped at the chance.

"Okay, now turn back to the mirror, and this time concentrate only on your eyes," Gary ordered. "Don't look at anything else. Not your hair. Not your shirt. Just your eyes."

Shelly turned toward the mirror above the sink. This time, Gary noticed she had looked directly into her own eyes. In a few seconds, Shelly started to smile a little. Her smile then grew into a wide grin. Her eyes suddenly lit up.

Gary saw the transformation happening right in front of him. His mom had come so far already. She was getting past this last hurdle in her transformation. He knew it.

Shelly giggled. She brought her hands up to her mouth and started shaking. Not from fear, but from the extreme happiness and joy that Gary had never seen. His mom was giggling like a schoolgirl.

"Oh my goodness." Shelly said it excitedly. "I can't believe I am actually looking at myself. I just can't believe it."

"Mom, you have such warm and kind eyes. I am so proud of you." Gary complimented Shelly while resting his hands on her shoulders. He called upstairs for Jessica.

"Honey!" Gary yelled upstairs. "Come here, quick. You have to see this."

Gary turned back to Shelly, still looking into the mirror at her eyes, smiling like never before. Jessica rushed downstairs, and Gary quickly filled her in on what was happening. She put her arm around Shelly's shoulders.

"Mom, your eyes are so warm and kind. You have loving eyes. I am so proud that you can finally look at them." Jessica said.

Shelly leaned forward, getting closer to the mirror. She could not stop smiling and giggling. Gary knew she had just crossed perhaps the last major hurdle in her miraculous recovery. A recovery that just weeks ago was unthinkable.

"I could never look at myself in the mirror." Shelly said, while still giggling. She was shaking from the excited energy. "I always thought my face was fat and ugly. I was convinced it was too wide, and I could never look at myself." Shelly said this with tears in her eyes. Tears not from sadness but from happiness and joy so great that one can't help but marvel at her transformation.

Gary and Jessica continued to give Shelly words of encouragement. She couldn't seem to pull herself away from the mirror. All those years of negative feelings were released at that moment. At eighty-two years old, Shelly Murphy could finally look into her own eyes in the mirror. She had released all these negative emotions and feelings that had been bottled up over the decades.

None of this could have been possible without the

steps she had taken at Brooke's house and Liz's help in making her realize she was needed and loved.

After what seemed like an eternity, Shelly emerged from the bathroom as a new woman, with Gary and Jessica following behind her. She had made remarkable strides before this, but now she was complete. Shelly Murphy had crossed that last hurdle.

She had to call her sister. Brooke needed to know about this. She spent the next several minutes telling Brooke about what Gary did for her. About how he got her into the bathroom to get her to look at herself in the mirror. She told Brooke about how she could not stop looking at herself and giggled like a schoolgirl.

Brooke was ecstatic. She was so proud of her big sister.

"Brooke, I couldn't have made it to this point and gotten through this without your help. Gary told me he couldn't have made this work with the mirror if you hadn't put me through that program and everything," Shelly said.

"Well, bless his heart," Brooke replied. "Shelly! You know this was a team effort, right? Gary, myself, Liz, you, and God. We couldn't have done it if you didn't let yourself be helped."

They continued to talk for a little while longer. Brooke continued to speak about her amazement at Shelly's progress. She told Shelly that most people have to take several months to make the same progress she had made in only a couple of weeks.

Later that day, Shelly walked into the bathroom. After

she came out, she marched over to Gary, beaming like a little kid, and said, "I looked at myself in the mirror again. I not only stood there and looked at myself, I stared at myself, and I liked what I saw in the reflection.

Gary was so proud of her. "Mom, I think your recovery is pretty much complete. I can't believe how far you have come in such a short time."

"Gary, I don't think I have ever felt this good and I owe it to you, to Brooke, to Liz, and most of all, to God. I think he helped set this whole thing in motion and put everything in place."

"I agree," Gary replied.

During the late afternoon, Gary, Shelly, Jessica, and Rylie drove to the local grocery store where Rylie and Jeff work. Jeff worked that day, so they thought they would see him and get a few things for dinner. When they finished shopping, all four of them walked out and got in the car. The parking spot in front of the car was empty. Gary had backed out instead of going forward through the empty parking spot.

Shelly commented, "You know, in the past, before this trip out here, I would have asked why don't you just drive forward. But after what you guys and Brooke and Liz helped me with, I don't even feel the need."

"You would always make suggestions to me about doing things differently than what I was doing. I always hated that." Gary replied.

"I know. I used to do that with Jason and Melanie. Neither of them liked it, either. I always thought I was helping by suggesting other ways to do things, but I guess I wasn't. Brooked said it was part of the co-dependency problem. I can see that now," Shelly had said.

She continued. "Jason used to take a longer way back home, and Melanie would drive a little further to get to Columbia City. I used to always get on them about going the longer way. Now I see why it would irritate them."

As Gary drove out of the parking lot of the grocery store, he replied to his mom. "I'm glad you realize that now, but back then, did you ever think that there was a reason that Jason and Melanie took the longer way? Perhaps Jason liked to drive that route for sentimental reasons or because he felt more comfortable with it. Maybe Melanie took the longer route to Columbia City because it made her feel more comfortable, or she could've had a close call on the shorter route."

"I never thought of those things back then. In my mind, I was always right and thought they could do better by using my suggestions." Shelly replied. "I see that now, and to tell the truth, what I know now would have irritated me as well."

"Back there at the parking spot, I didn't go forward because the lane in the middle goes right in front of the door to the grocery store. It sometimes gets busy with people going in and coming out. By backing up and going the way I did, there would be a lot fewer people in that area." Gary explained.

Shelly nodded. "Yep. I understand all of that now and I could have suggested that you go forward, but I didn't. I just explained it to you to show you how far I have come and what I've learned."

"No problem. I knew what you were talking about," Gary replied.

After they arrived home, Rylie suggested they go to their favorite thrift store. It was part of a large church in a nearby town. Most of the people who worked there knew Gary and Jessica. They all agreed to go. Jeff was still at work at the supermarket and would not get off until later that day.

All four got into the small, white Honda CR-V. Gary drove, Shelly sat in the front, and Jessica and Rylie sat in the back. While driving to the thrift store, Jessica, who sat behind Shelly, noticed the back of her neck under the gold chain with her favorite cross.

"Mom, did you realize the chain is turning your neck green? It must not be good quality." Jessica informed Shelly.

Shelly leaned forward a bit to turn and glanced back at Jessica. She grabbed her chain and replied. "Is it really? Oh darn. This is my favorite necklace. Or at least the cross is."

"Yes, it is. It's not too bad, but it's turning your skin green. The thrift store has several chains we can sort through." Jessica suggested.

"I hope I can find a good one," Shelly replied.

When they got to the thrift store, Gary headed for the hardware and electronics section. Rylie walked back to the clothes, and Shelly and Jessica walked over to look at the necklaces and chains in the display case by the cash register. Shelly hoped to find the right chain for her cross.

Jessica was more familiar with the chains there, so she looked and found one that might work. She asked the thrift store employee to get the necklace out of the case for her. She noticed it did not have a cross on it. Instead, there was a small oval-shaped pendant with writing on it. Jessica looked closely and read the words. She smiled and called for Shelly.

"Mom. I think I found one. You've got to read this," Jessica said.

Shelly leaned in close. She was not too interested in any pendants. Shelly wanted a chain for her necklace. Maybe she could take off the pendant and use the chain.

"Let me see it," Shelly said as she reached for the necklace.

Jessica handed it to her, and Shelly held the pendant close to her face to read the small writing. Her readers on her glasses helped a lot. She read out loud.

Find Joy in the Journey.

Shelly smiled and even chuckled a bit. She turned to Jessica. "Oh my. It's like this necklace was meant just for me. I found real joy on this journey. Is this fate or what?" Shelly had said.

"It was meant to be, Mom. It was the first one I picked up." Jessica said while smiling and rubbing Shelly's back with her left hand.

Shelly was still smiling. She felt it was God's hand leading her and Jessica to this particular necklace.

"I've got to show Gary and Rylie," Shelly said. She took the necklace and started walking to find them. Fortunately, she found them close to each other and walked up to them.

"Gary, Rylie! I've got to show you this." Shelly said this with a big smile on her face.

"Look what Jessica found. This was the first one she picked out."

Gary and his daughter, Rylie, leaned in, took the pendant, and looked at it together. Gary read it out loud. *Find Joy in the Journey.*

Gary and Rylie smiled and looked at Shelly. Rylie spoke first. "Grandma, this is so weird. It's like it was meant just for you."

Gary followed up jokingly, "Hey, you took my line."

They all laughed. Then Gary continued. "My goodness, mom. It's like everything has been falling into place perfectly on this trip. Now you've got a reminder with this necklace."

Shelly took out her phone to call Brooke. She told the others what she was doing. After selecting Brooke's number in the contacts section, the phone rang on the other end.

"Hey Shelly. What're you up to?" Brooked answered, seeing that it was her sister on the caller ID.

"Well, I've got to tell you about what Jessica found for me at the thrift store."

Shelly began telling the story about how Jessica saw that her old necklace was turning her skin green and that she needed to get a new one. She continued to talk about the necklace at the store and how it was the first one Jessica had spotted. When Shelly read the little quote on the necklace pendant, Jessica and

Gary could hear the burst of laughter from Brooke. She couldn't believe the message on the pendant and agreed that it was meant for Shelly to have it.

After Shelly and the others left the store and got home, they continued to talk about the necklace and its message until dinner. When Jeff got home from work at the supermarket, they told him about what had happened. He thought it was neat, but being a typical teenage boy, he showed little excitement.

Shelly and the others had mainly talked about family and news topics of the day, along with eating Jessica's wonderful home-cooked food. Shelly, along with Gary and Rylie, went through more pictures of Shelly's parents, grandparents, great-grandparents, and other relatives. Some photos date back to the very early 1900s. Several photographs were of Shelly's mom and dad riding horses on the ranch.

It was early morning on the last day of Shelly's trip. Gary and Jessica were taking Shelly to the Spokane train station late that night. Her train was scheduled to leave around midnight. Brooke was coming over for lunch and to say goodbye to her big sister.

A NEW WOMAN

Shelly woke up a little later than usual. She has been sleeping better these last few days than she has ever slept before. She has loved her stay in Idaho. It changed her life and most likely saved it. She was ready to get back home and start living life.

Shelly packed up most of her things in the suitcase and small bag before everyone else woke up. She left out just a few of her toiletries to use during the day. By the time she walked upstairs after packing, Gary and Jessica were already awake.

"Good morning, mom." Gary and Jessica both said.

"Good morning, you guys."

"How did you sleep?" Gary asked.

"Better than I've slept in ages," Shelly answered.

Jessica moved into the kitchen to begin breakfast. "So, mom. What do you want for your last breakfast here? How about pancakes?"

"That sounds good. We can all have some," Shelly replied.

Jessica pulled out their home-made pancake mix from the plastic zip-lock bag. Gary helped and got the milk and vinegar. The recipe they used for pancakes was the best they ever had. Gary had searched, unsuccessfully, for a good recipe and was about to give up on the search until he found this one. He was not looking for a new recipe, but he came across this one that looked promising.

It was a different recipe than most of the others. This one involved souring the milk with vinegar. They have used no other pancake recipe since then.

At the dinner table, they gathered around for their last breakfast together during this trip. The talk was pleasant and focused on Shelly's time in Idaho.

"What time is aunt Brooke planning on coming over today?" Jessica asked. "I know she's coming for lunch."

"I think she said around eleven this morning. Brooke wanted to spend a little time but has to leave around one in the afternoon for a couple of appointments." Shelly answered.

At a little before eleven in the morning, the doorbell rang. Everyone knew who it was. Gary went and opened the door for Brooke. She had little Jonah on the leash.

"Hi, I hope you don't mind me bringing Jonah," Brooke said.

Jonah was barking and excited to be at his second home. He barked until Rylie bent down to pet him. Gary and Jessica had watched Jonah at different times at their house. He was familiar with the layout and made himself comfortable once he calmed down.

"Come on in and have a seat," Gary said.

Shelly and Brooke said hello and gave each other hugs. Jessica, who was upstairs fixing lunch in the kitchen, came down to greet Brooke. "Hi, aunt Brooke. Can I get you some coffee?"

"Yes. That sounds nice. Cream, no sugar."

"Okay. Mom, do you want a refill? Jessica asked Shelly.

Shelly lifted her cup to show she had plenty. "No, I have enough. Thank you, anyway."

Once lunch was ready, Jessica called everyone to the table. Jeff was the only one not there. He was at school. Jessica fixed a simple lunch of home-made chicken noodle soup, salad with carrots; croutons; salad dressing and a side of home-made breadsticks. Everyone enjoyed the lunch.

Brooke spoke to Shelly at the table. "Shelly, I can't believe how different you are now. It's like you're a whole new person. Even more so than when you left my place."

The others sitting at the table agreed with Brooke. Shelly smiled at the compliment.

"Who would have ever thought I could change this much in this short amount of time after all I went through and what I felt? Let's not forget all that you went through and how well you've come through it. Jessica was right about what she said to you at the coffee shop." Shelly said.

Brooke continued, "I think God stepped in right from the very beginning. Just like the way Liz mentioned, he sent dad to you in his drunken state after the last incident with Bill to keep you from doing something bad. I believe God set everything in motion. For example, keeping me from visiting you in Indiana when I drove to Minnesota. We wouldn't have had any real time to talk with each other and do the program with the neighbors stopping by. To Liz for making that surprise visit when you needed her most. And finally, with what Gary and Jessica had helped you do regarding that last hurdle with the mirror,"

Jessica interrupted, "Aunt Brooke, thank you, but Gary had helped Mom the most with the mirror."

"Well, you were there to support her while she was going through it, and from what she said, you helped encourage her," Brooke added. "Without either myself, Liz, or Gary, even if two of us were helping, it would not have worked to transform you like a butterfly from a cocoon. I truly believe that."

Just then, Gary butted in with a funny comment. "Yeah! An eighty-two-year-old butterfly." Everyone laughed, including Shelly.

Brooke continued talking after the laughter died down. "God had a huge hand in making everything happen as it should have. I must say that we were all worried about how you were before you got here. Those notes you showed me in your diary reaffirmed that we all made the right decision by talking you into coming out here."

Shelly agreed with Brooke. She could look back and see how bad she had gotten, and that she was ready to give up and pass on.

"I have all of you to thank for this. All the worries I used to have are gone. I no longer worry about what other people think of me and no longer feel guilty about mom's death or Bill's death. I am going to live for myself and not let others get me down. It's not that I am the happiest I have ever been. I had some great and happy times with Jason. I think it's because I am the most content and at peace with myself that I have ever been in my entire life." Shelly professed.

Shelly gave a brief testimonial to everyone at the dinner table, which captivated them. They all expressed their happiness and joy that Shelly was a changed woman. Just then, Brooke looked at the time on the clock on the wall next to the dining table. It was getting close to one o'clock.

"Well, Shelly. It's about time for me to go." Jonah knew when it was time to leave. He got up and stood next to Brooke in anticipation of leaving. They walked down the stairs to the front door. Gary opened the door, and they all walked with Brooke and Jonah to her car.

"Come here." Brooke pulled Shelly in for a big hug.

Both of them got a few tears in their eyes. Tears of joy from the emotional journey they had taken in these last three or four weeks together. The healing that both of them had gone through during Shelly's stay in Idaho.

"I'm going to miss you. We need to get together more often. What you did for me to help me heal is something I will never forget and that I will always cherish." Shelly spoke to Brooke as she wiped some tears from her face.

Brooke moved in for another hug. "One hug wasn't enough, sis."

After they hugged each other a second time, Brooke got Jonah into the backseat of the car, and then she got into the driver's side. She backed the car up, and once she was on the street, she looked over at Shelly, and the others waved and blew kisses.

Shelly spent the rest of the day relaxing and resting. Rylie said she wanted to go along when Gary and Jessica took Shelly to the train station. Jeff spent part of the time visiting with his grandma. He had school the next day, so he would stay home to sleep.

After dinner, reflecting on her trip, and relaxing in the living room, it was finally time to load the car up with Shelly's bags. Jeff and Gary loaded them into the car. They left a little early so they could be at the train station in plenty of time. Gary had been checking the inbound train to make sure it was going to be on time into Spokane.

Shelly gave her grandson, Jeff, a big hug. "You are getting big. I have to reach way up now to hug you."

Shelly said. Jeff just smiled. "You were always a cute boy, and now you're a handsome young man." Shelly complimented Jeff. It made him smile even more. A little redness appeared in his cheeks.

The ride to the Spokane train station was pleasant. There wasn't too much traffic on the interstate this late in the evening. There were a lot of cars in the train station parking lot, but Gary had no problem finding a spot.

He and Rylie carried most of the bags inside the terminal. They checked on the train's status at the front desk. The man at the desk was polite and helpful and knew about the status of the train. He said that it was going to be on time.

They then headed to the waiting area, where Shelly could wait to board the train when it was ready. They didn't have to wait very long. The announcement came. Shelly and the rest got up to head to the boarding pass area. Gary took care of most of the bags. He always joked that one of his jobs in the family was being a pack mule.

Gary stopped at the gate and asked the attendants if they could escort Shelly to the train. They said it would be no problem at all and to tell the ticket takers in each section about going on the train to help Shelly.

They found the section Shelly was going to be in. Even though the three of them were escorting her onto the train and to her seat, they hugged each other outside the train car. The space inside would be a little tight.

Following the women, Gary had brought Shelly's suitcase and little bag to her seat. She had her laptop in it and other things she would need for the trip back. Her assigned seat was in the upstairs part of the train car. Even though she was a fit eighty-two-year-old, she didn't want to make several trips up and down the stairs to the designated luggage bins.

Shelly said a quick goodbye to Gary, Jessica, and Rylie and watched them leave. She was on the opposite side of the platform and could not look out the window at them from the train.

As the passenger train prepared to depart, Shelly got ready and settled in for a night's sleep. It was a little after midnight, and she was tired. It didn't take her long to fall asleep once the train started moving. The subtle motion of the cars on the tracks lulled her to a fast sleep.

When she awoke, the sun was coming up near the horizon. Not too bright yet, but enough light spread out over the land from the low sun in the eastern sky to see the surrounding landscape. She figured she must be somewhere in the low-lying mountains of Montana, east of Glacier National Park.

Shelly didn't know it, but Jessica had packed some snacks and drinks for her the night before. She opened her bag and found a plastic container with two choco-late chip muffins, bottled water, and a small assortment of other snacks. There were some napkins in the con-tainer, too. She smiled and shook her head in pleasant surprise.

Shelly thought to herself. *There she goes again, spoil-ing me.* She loved her kids and their spouses. They have all been so good to her. It took this trip for her to realize it.

After she finished her muffin and had some water from a small plastic bottle, Shelly sat back in her chair and gazed out the window. She reflected on the healing and positive changes that happened to her. Not just healing her emotionally, but healing deep down to her soul.

Eighty-two-year-old Shelly Murphy looked out the window of the train and smiled. She was going home a new and reborn woman. Even at her age, she was looking forward to a new life and what lay ahead.

EPILOGUE

After returning home from her life-changing and life-saving trip to Idaho, eighty-two-year-old Shelly Murphy's daughter, Melanie, and her son-in-law, Matthew, picked her up at the train station. They had a forty-minute drive back to their town. Melanie could notice the profound change in her mom. She saw the light in her eyes.

On the way home in the car, Shelly shared with them the program she went through with Brooke and what Liz and Gary had done for her. Melanie was excited to see her mom looking so happy. She worried about her mom before this trip, as did the rest of the family.

Two weeks after returning home from Idaho, Shelly gathered several of the residents from her senior apartment complex into the community room. She was used to listening to all their stories and problems, but she told them she wanted to share something incredible with them. Most residents at the apartment complex noticed how she looked since her return and commented on it, but none of them knew what had changed her.

Shelly stood in front of the group, and they all got quiet.

"I would like to tell you my testimony of what has happened to me in my life. Of what I went through, that made me unhappy on the inside and eventually led me to almost give up."

Shelly spoke for two and a half hours, telling her story. It included the period with her mom, her time with her first husband, Bill, and what he did to her, leading up to watching both her dad and, several years later, her second husband die of cancer. She shared with them how she was ready to give up on life and wanted the Lord to take her soon. She felt she had nothing more to live for.

Many of the women listening to Shelly shed tears in their eyes through most of her testimony. They all stayed quiet and listened while Shelly told her story. She spent about the last thirty minutes telling the residents about what happened to her during the Idaho trip. The surprise visit by her daughter, Liz; renouncements and the sudden feeling of warmth and love she had after reading them, the bathroom mirror episode that her son, Gary, helped her through.

Shelly finished the testimony by saying that she believed God had a major role in saving her life. Many of the women in the room who were still crying came up to Shelly afterward and hugged her. They told her how wonderful she looked and how they could see the change. Many told her that her testimony and her story had affected them. They've had things happen to them in the past that they never got over. They saw hope through Shelly Murphy.

In the year since the trip, Shelly has not wavered in her happiness or her contentment. She is closer to God than she has ever been. Her kids, who were worried that she might regress to her old self, are now convinced that their mom has changed permanently for the better. They have never seen their mom so happy and content as they do now. Shelly has had many of the people to whom she gave her testimony ask her to help them in little groups at the apartment complex. She gladly accepted, and with the help of Brooke's material from the program, she has been holding weekly meetings in her little apartment.

About eight months after Shelly returned to Indiana, she wrote a well-thought-out letter to her kids and sent it to each of them via email. She wanted to express how she felt and how she had changed for the better.

To My kids

Oh boy! I don't know where to begin. I guess it was just last summer. I was so depressed and broken. I had so many regrets about how my life was and what I put you kids through.

I felt I was the worst mother ever. The only good thing I believed I did was to get you kids to church as much as I could. We weren't a stable family, that's for sure. What with all the places we had lived in during the first fifteen years of marriage.

I am so happy that you three kids have lived at the

same place for so long as adults and kept your kids in the same school system all their lives. I'm so glad you didn't follow the example of your parents moving all the time.

When I traveled to Idaho, a miracle happened to me. I could never really look at myself in a mirror because I always saw an old, ugly face staring back at me. God had refreshed, restored, and renewed my heart, and now when I look in the mirror, I like what I see. I had such a great healing while I was with Brooke and Liz at Brooke's place and while I was at Gary and Jessica's.

My stay at Brooke's was the first time that we were ever really able to get to know each other and learn what each of us went through after our mom died. We even learned more about each of our marriages.

I still often wonder why I didn't take Brooke in and raise her myself. I didn't know that she was bounced around to different family members in her childhood. She didn't have a good life. I am so sorry that it took me into my 80s to really know my sister.

I guess that's the reason for this letter. There are just you three kids, and Melanie. Please stay in contact with each other and with the nieces and nephews. Don't wait until you're my age because we missed out on family time.

I love the journey God has for me. I have joy, hope, and faith, and I refuse to be discouraged. I'm not sure what God has planned for me in the future, but right now, my calendar is full almost every day.

I started a ladies' group here at my apartment. I prayed I would get at least five gals, and ten showed up. Three others were sick. That would have been thirteen, lol. We are going to have a women's bible group this summer.

You know, all I had to learn for God's plan of salvation was to believe in Him as the one who bore your sin, died in your place, was buried, and whom God had resurrected.

His resurrection assured that the believer can claim everlasting life when Jesus is received as the Savior. Yep, he saved a sinner like me. I'm sure you may remember that from the Nazarene church.

But you know, I now have peace in my heart. I don't get discouraged. I have patience. I have love for everyone. I love you kids so much. I'm just going to see what God has planned for me now.

I am just so proud of each of you. I brag about my kids all the time. You have made good choices in your life. Not everyone has had a childhood like you kids had and turned out so great. I am not going to ramble on anymore. I think you get the picture. I am so happy. There is much more to tell you all, but I don't remember what. Plus, I can't find my notes. I am sending this same message to all of you kids.

I love you all very much.

Mom

Since Shelly left Idaho, her sister, Brooke, has started holding meetings and group therapy in her home through her church. The church Brooke attends was so impressed with how she had healed and how affected she was by helping her sister heal, they asked her if she could host groups in her home. Brooke continues to guide people through the program that helped her and Shelly heal. She finds that helping others also helps her.

Brooke and her divorced second husband, Mark, have been on friendly terms. They are taking things slowly, but there is talk of reconciliation.

INSPIRATIONAL QUOTES

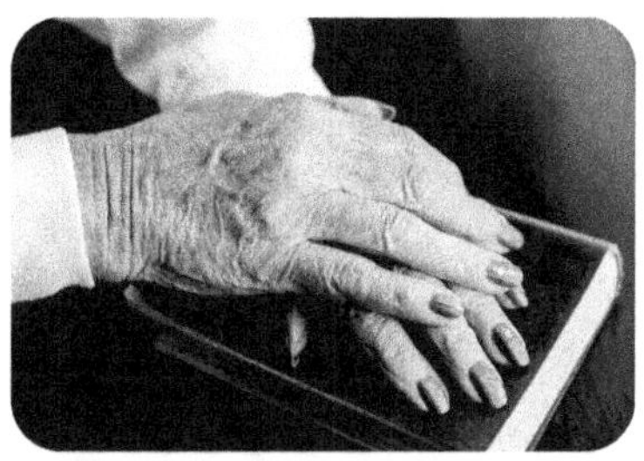

"Heal your soul. The healing of your body and mind will follow."

Anonymous

"Healing is only successful if you allow yourself to be healed."

Anonymous

"A healing heart is good medicine, but a crushed spirit dries up the bones."

Proverbs 17:22

THE AUTHOR'S BIOGRAPHY

Gregory Johnston lives with his family in beautiful north Idaho. He is a published photographer whose photos have sold around the world in stock photo agencies, magazines, calendars, and several online articles and publications.